One Man's Treasure

by

Eva Fox Mate

The Wild Rose Press, Inc.
PO Box 708
Adams Basin, NY 14410-0708
Visit us at www.thewildrosepress.com

Publishing History
First Edition, 2024
Trade Paperback ISBN 978-1-5092-5693-8
Digital ISBN 978-1-5092-5694-5

Hughes Brothers Trilogy, Book 1
Published in the United States of America

Dedication

To Ed, Anna, and Sam,
with my everlasting love and gratitude

Acknowledgments

Writing is often considered a solitary pursuit but, thankfully, I haven't found it to be so. This book (and my sanity) benefitted greatly from the first-class critiquing and cheerleading of my friend and fellow writer, Romy Sommer. I thank you from the bottom of my heart, girl!

In addition, I am grateful for the writing sprint pals I see each morning during the work week. Maureen, Ellen, Sherry, Allorianna, Lauren, and Joel deserve fond shout-outs for supporting me through the ups and downs of this writing life.

Of course, I also owe more than I can say to the wonderful and supportive folks at The Wild Rose Press.

Last, but certainly not least, I want to thank my family—near and far, two-legged and four, by blood and by marriage—for their constant support. You're the very best and I love each and every one of you very much!

Prologue

"Did you find it?" The harsh voice on the other end of the phone sent a shudder through the man's thin frame.

"No, I just got here. I was held up—"

"I don't care," the voice rasped. "I'm paying you handsomely to find it, so find it."

The man chafed against the order but remained silent. He hated being told what to do, but it was true—the money that came with this job was fantastic.

He rubbed his temples with the thumb and middle finger of his free hand. "Okay. I'll search this evening once most—"

Again, the voice erupted, louder this time. "That's too late. I want an update by noon."

"That's not possible." The man squinted across the green at a large, colonial-style, red brick building. "The campus is crawling with people right now."

"That's your problem. Noon. Or you piss me off and don't get paid. Not a good situation for you. People who piss me off often meet with…difficulties." A sinister crack of laughter echoed down the line.

The man gripped the phone until his knuckles turned white. "Right. Noon. At the same place?" Best not to poke the bear.

"Yes." The line clicked dead.

Pocketing his phone with a sigh, he raised the dark

hood of his sweatshirt. It bore the name of the campus he stood on, not the one he had attended several years before. A black canvas backpack and a pair of aviator sunglasses completed his outfit.

He'd been hired for this job because he was a chameleon, an ordinary-looking man who blended into any surroundings. He preferred to think of himself as a master actor, playing whatever part gave him the salary his talent deserved.

He walked slowly toward the massive building, where students scrambled like ants around an ant hole, and brainstormed how to play this scene. Usually, he pulled his jobs before or after the workday. Less people, less chance of being caught.

But his new employer, a very powerful man, was known for his impatience and it would be suicide to make him mad. So, this job would be done before noon.

No matter what.

Chapter One

She wouldn't beg.

Anything else, yes. As long as it was legal. Callie Wallis struggled with the admission almost as much as she struggled with the history building's worn concrete steps. There had been plenty of desperate times in her life, but this made the top three. Leaving tonight without a solution wasn't an option. She couldn't tell her sister, Gretchen, that she'd have to leave her home.

So Callie wouldn't beg. But she wouldn't take "no" for an answer, either.

Before entering the sprawling building, she inhaled the crisp fall air. She loved this time of year. After a hot, lethargic summer, the campus was reborn in the fall. She loved the hectic scramble of students, trying to make it to classes on time. Loved the beauty of the elderly trees, transformed by the falling temperatures into a riot of scarlet and yellow leaves. She loved the final glimpses of sun before the gray of winter descended. Most of all, she loved knowing she would soon see her sexy-as-hell boss after a long, lonely summer.

Nope. She wouldn't go there. There was no time to indulge in pointless romantic longings today. Today was cold, hard reality and nothing else.

Sighing, she caught the edge of the closing door and joined the steady stream of people inside the musty old building. *Adam.* She'd take a year in the dentist's chair over the conversation she faced.

But she couldn't put it off any longer. She'd had most of the summer to stew over it, to survey her options, or lack thereof. Time to lay it all out and see what happened. Roll the dice. She had learned a thing or three about Adam Hughes in the five years she'd worked for him. Topping the list was his love of cool, calm, rational thought. Reason would be her watchword.

Avoid drama at any cost.

"Do we have a baby yet, Rob?" Habit as well as affection dictated Callie's stop alongside the wooden security and information desk, where the gray-haired, stoop-shouldered security guard had sat for the better part of forty years.

"We do indeed." He poked at his cellphone, beaming with pride. "Here's my great-granddaughter, born yesterday afternoon. Named her Roberta, though I told them they shouldn't have."

"Congratulations!" Callie pressed a hand to her chest as she gazed at the photo of Rob holding a pink-cheeked, swaddled newborn. "Oh, she's beautiful." With effort, she swatted away the tug of longing that struck. She had enough on her plate without adding a ticking biological clock to the pile. "I hope everyone's doing well?"

"You bet." He took his phone back, then slipped it into his breast pocket. "How's my favorite personal assistant doing today?"

She forced a smile. "Fine, thanks."

"Boss back today?"

"Of course." She eyed the chaos of students surrounding them. "He wouldn't miss the start of another school year."

"Where'd he get off to this summer?"

"A cabin along the coast in Maine. Got another book written."

Rob shook his head. "It'll be another winner. That man knows how to write a first-rate thriller. Last one had me up half the night."

Callie chuckled. Every one of Adam's novels about a 1950s spy named Wolfe Bridges was well crafted and nearly impossible to put down.

"Yes, this one's just as bad—and by bad, I mean good. I've been busy all summer with his edits. I'm glad school has started. Now that he's back to being a plain old professor, my workload might slow down a bit." She spoke good-naturedly but was only half joking.

"I hope so. You work too hard." Rob crooked a finger at a confused-looking student. "Looks like I'd better get back to work myself. You have yourself a good day, Callie, you hear?"

"You, too." Her smile came more easily this time.

Chats with the old man always brightened her day. However, the brightness was short-lived. Her smile evaporated as she began her slow climb up the wide wooden stairway to the second floor. The uncertainty of her future loomed larger with every step.

Logic. That was the key. If she presented things sensibly, Adam might agree. After all, the man wasn't an ogre. Although he would never admit it, he wasn't quite as cold as he pretended.

Stoic, yes. Emotionally damaged, certainly. But she'd caught the emotion flickering in his gray-blue eyes whenever she rose unsteadily to her feet or seesawed her way up a flight of stairs. It wasn't pity. She understood that look too well to misinterpret it.

It was…understanding. Unspoken acknowledgment

that he fathomed, better than most, how much the accident had stolen from her six long years ago.

How time had flown. The fact she'd walked—okay, hobbled—into his office five years ago and won the job as his assistant still had her pinching herself at times.

Funny how motivating a guilty conscience was.

Now, her job, begun as a penance, was a fulfilling partnership. The best five years of her life.

And today, you risk it all.

She reached the second-floor landing with the usual small sense of victory. After four hip surgeries, she took the win mastery of the stairs represented. A quick swim through the waves of students brought her to an imposing door bearing a discreet brass plaque. *Dr. Adam C. Hughes, J.D., PhD.* Home sweet home, eight to five, five days a week.

The door's lack of any other decoration was indicative of its occupant's humility. Adam hated the limelight and avoided undue attention the way a cat avoided rocking chairs. However, when you were the grandson of a US president and the son of the current Chief Justice of the US Supreme Court, keeping a low profile was next to impossible. Given his loathing of all things ostentatious, she was surprised Adam still used his real name.

She plopped her large, woven bag down on the arm of one of the hallway benches and rooted around for her office access card. It had a bad habit of falling to the bottom of her cavernous purse. Over the years, her well-intentioned but not very imaginative boss had gifted her with a store's worth of lanyards—plain, sparkly, colorful, bland—to save her from searching through what he teasingly called "the black hole." She would sooner die than reveal she found the cords difficult to wear when she was on the move, given her uneven gait.

Her peripheral vision was snagged by a man in jeans and a dark hoody, slouched at the other end of the bench. A nod in his direction got no response. He might be asleep, his eyes hidden behind a pair of mirrored, aviator-style sunglasses. She'd seen it before. A student who'd partied a little too hard the night before.

"Ha!" Victorious at last, she withdrew the lanyard Adam had given her for her last birthday and slipped it around her neck.

This one was pretty, with an ombre purple tassel on the end that all but hid the ugly key card. The tassel danced as she placed the card on the sensor. At the mechanical snick of the lock, the man on the bench stood and ambled around behind her as she pushed the door open. Hmm. Not sleeping then. Had she forgotten an early appointment?

"Be right with you." She hurried to her desk in the office's small anteroom.

Only human, every now and then she forgot to record something, but it rankled every time. She was both old- and new-school when it came to Adam's appointments, writing them in long-hand on a large desk calendar as well as typing them into the computer app they shared. Check and double-check was her mantra.

"No worries."

Her gaze narrowed when the man closed the hallway door. As moves went, it was hardly deadly, but a frisson of fear ran down her spine. Something wasn't right.

"I'm sorry." Stepping away from the desk, she straightened to her full five feet ten inches, an inch or two taller than the slightly built man. "I don't have any appointment down. Is Dr. Hughes expecting you?"

The man unzipped his black backpack and reached inside. "You could say that."

It was the last thing she heard as pain radiated through her head and everything went dark.

****

"Have you seen it yet?" Adam Hughes slammed his computer shut and slipped off the chrome-and-leather barstool. He gave it a healthy kick back into its spot under the kitchen counter.

"Oh, yeah," his younger brother, Mason, cackled on the other end of the phone. "It's viral, man. Famous recluse, Adam Hughes, caught in a major lip-lock. That was an X-rated kiss you and Angela shared. Mum and Dad are thrilled you're finally getting out there again!"

"They'll be disappointed, then, because it's not like that and you know it." Adam wanted nothing to do with Angela Carson, or any other woman for that matter. That Angela had staged the whole thing—paparazzi, front-page photo, everything—was no surprise. "There's a new Bridges movie in the works, and that viper wants to play the femme fatale. Thinks that if she's my girlfriend, she'll get the part. Everywhere I go there she is, waiting to pounce. She even followed me to Maine. I can't get rid of her."

"Pain in your ass she may be, bro, but there's history there. And I'm not talking about the snooze-worthy kind you teach."

"Very funny." Adam popped another pod into his coffee maker, aligned his cup, then pressed the brew button. Within seconds, the invigorating aroma of the coffee pervaded the room, and he breathed it in like a drowning man gulped air. "That's *ancient* history." The college fling he and Angela had enjoyed for a hot minute had been a mistake. "I was young and stupid, and she was beautiful and willing." And ice cold to the core.

"Well, she's still beautiful, and movie or no, I think she wants you bad, big brother."

Adam blew on his coffee before taking a tentative sip. *Ahhh.*

"You're such a turd," he said, with brotherly affection. "Sometimes, it's hard to believe you have a medical degree. Whatever Angela thinks, it's not mutual." He took another cautious sip. "Definitely. Not. Mutual. It's getting old, Mace. I'd do almost anything to get her off my case."

"Well, you could always fly out to Vegas and marry a woman you barely know." Amusement lifted Mason's voice. "Worked for me. Priss and I are old news now. Just another boring old married couple."

Adam laughed at the thought of his new sister-in-law. "Right. Like Priscilla's ever boring."

"She's constantly amazing," Mason agreed, with the fervor of a besotted husband. "Just saying, it's good to be off the market."

Adam left the kitchen, crossing into the ultra-modern, high-gloss white living room of his third floor penthouse apartment. With his back to the panoramic views of Washington, DC, he stared over at the fireplace.

Its stark, black mantel held only one thing—a framed black-and-white photograph of an unbelievably beautiful woman. He didn't mean her dark hair, expressive eyes, and high cheek bones, although those attributes added up to model-like external beauty.

Mallory, his late wife, had been as gorgeous on the inside as she had been outside. More so, even. Kind, considerate, supportive, patient. Oh, so patient with his sorry ass. If only he could tell her how much he loved her one more time.

As the usual pangs of sadness and regret tugged at his stomach, he raised his mug toward her likeness before resolutely turning his mind back to the subject at hand. "You know I'm not on the market. I'll *never* be back on the market. Is it asking too much to work and live as I want, away from prying eyes?"

On the other end of the phone, Mason sighed. "News flash. You're a Hughes. For us, there's no such thing."

"Yeah, well, you know me." Adam set his mug down and ran a finger across the smooth glass preserving Mallory's image. "Always wanting what I can't have."

His phone vibrated, and he lifted it away from his ear to read the incoming text message.

Shit.

He hit the phone's speaker button. "Mace, I gotta go. There's been a break-in at the university. Security just texted me, and Callie's been hurt."

"Is it serious?" In an instant, Mason flipped from jerk younger brother to concerned medico.

Adam rushed through the rest of the text. "Knock on the head, maybe a concussion. They're sending her to the hospital for tests."

"Do you want company?"

Adam's heart swelled. Mason knew too well that Adam avoided hospitals like the plague. With a slight shake of his head, he swallowed a deep breath. "No, it's okay. I'm a big boy."

****

Oh, those eyes. Those deep, brooding, stormy-sea eyes.

"Gorgeous eyes. Drown in them…" Callie mumbled before allowing her eyelids to fall again.

"Callie? That's it. Come on, wake up."

With great reluctance, she opened her eyes again, but only half-mast. Even the dimly lit room sent cymbals clanging in her head.

"Adam?" *What in the world is he doing here? He'll miss class, and he* never *misses a class. And where is here?*

She struggled to sit up, but another blinding flash of pain sent her reeling back against the softness. Keeping her head still, she patted around. *A bed.* She was in a bed and—yep, class or no class, her handsome, dark-haired boss leaned over her, concern radiating from his mesmerizing blue eyes.

As usual, the familiar sharp angles of Adam's face left her a little breathless. Despite the nagging sense there were other things she should be worrying about, she drank in the sight of him, her first for several months. *Mmmm.* He made her mouth water.

He was deliciously tall—about six-five— and…buff. So buff. He flashed that flirty dimple within the sculpted lines of his jaw, quirked his firm, kissable lips, and her heartrate jumped.

"Wait…where am I?"

There it was. *That* was what she should be focusing on. She wet her parched lips with her tongue without much success. What had she been eating? Cotton balls?

"What happened? Why aren't you at school?" She gazed up at him with something one notch down from panic clawing at her throat. "Why aren't *I* at school?"

The bed dipped as he sat on the edge of the mattress, taking care not to jostle her in the process. His sexy mouth split into a rueful smile, highlighting his perfect white teeth. "Because somebody conked you on the head. You're in the hospital."

"Hospital!" She slid all the way into panic. "No. I can't be in the hospital!"

Again, she levered herself up on to her elbows, only to be bombarded by waves of pain. Her stomach flip-flopped like a fish on dry land, and she sank back down again, cursing her weakness.

Adam reached out and, with endearing awkwardness, rested his hand on her shoulder. The move, innocent though it was, took her by surprise. Aside from handshakes or a hug among his own family, he never touched anyone. Ever. He was much too reserved. Her stomach rolled over again, but this time it had nothing to do with her injury and everything to do with her boss.

He smelled clean and woodsy, like a walk in a forest.

Easy, Killer. You've got better things to do than get all hot and bothered.

"I don't understand." That was understatement at its best. "Why in the world would somebody hit me?"

Eyes twinkling, Adam gave her another grin. "That's the billion-dollar question right now. Do you remember anything?"

Her mind drifted back over the morning. She'd gotten up, taken the subway to work, talked to Rob, then…nothing.

As if she weren't experiencing enough shock, Adam gave her a squeeze before releasing her shoulder. "It's okay, Cal. Don't force it. It'll come. We'll let the campus police figure it all out."

Sure, easy for him to say. He wasn't the one drawing a complete blank. Sighing, she looked around at the light green walls. Why were hospitals always green? Surely, someone could…

Oh, shit. What was she doing? Wasting her time lying here when it cost five hundred dollars a minute? She kicked the covers off and struggled up onto her elbows. The room did a slow-motion spin.

"Whoa. What do you think you're doing?"

Before she could even think about standing, Adam gathered up the discarded blankets and spread them over her once more. With a mighty shove, he tucked them firmly under the mattress. Great. Now she was trapped in a cocoon. An expensive cocoon she couldn't afford.

"Un-uh. Until the doctor says that knot on your head looks better, you aren't going anywhere." He tilted his head sideways and nodded. "It's a pretty good one."

She wiggled a hand free and raised it to her temple, but he caught her wrist before she made contact. God, he had fast hands.

Not necessarily a bad thing in a man.

Crap. The bump on her head must be worse than she thought.

"Trust me." He folded her arm across her stomach. "You've got a baseball-sized hematoma up there and ten stitches. You'll want to let the swelling go down before you start poking and prodding."

"No." She shook her head. *Whoops. Bad idea.* "No, *you* don't understand. I can't afford to be here."

He stared at her for a long moment, as if calculating how scrambled her brain might be. Which made two of them. "You can't afford *not* to be. This is the most alert you've been since I arrived twenty minutes ago. I overheard the nurses say you have a grade two concussion. That's serious. You'll stay overnight, at the very least."

"No." She gritted her teeth against the pain. "I literally can't afford it. The university cut my benefits. I need every dime I have, and then some, for Gretchen."

Frowning, he shook his head. "That can't be right. I thought the cuts only applied to part-time employees?"

She gave a choked laugh, then winced as more of the percussion section started up inside her head. "I *am* a part-time employee—they cut my hours as well."

Adam made a disbelieving sound and, with the confident air of a man accustomed to making things happen, reached into his suit jacket for his phone. "We'll see about that," he said, thumbing at the screen.

In lieu of shaking her head, she waved her hand dismissively, letting her arm flop back onto the bed, her fingers brushing the hard muscle of his thigh. Accident or not, it was an intimate touch that gave her more than a few sinful ideas.

She yanked her hand away faster than a kid caught fingering cookies in a jar, and shoved it back under the bedclothes. Head trauma or no, this nonsense had to stop.

"If you're calling President Garrison, don't bother." After five years, she predicted Adam's moves better than the world's best psychic. "I've been working on this for half the summer. Apparently, the university lost a ton of money during the pandemic, and he said there would be no exceptions, not even for you."

"Damn it." Adam slipped his phone back where it belonged, then turned and studied her again, irritation etching sharp lines in his handsome face. "Why am I just hearing about all this now?"

"I…you were busy finishing up the book, so I didn't want to bother you." Geez. It sounded lame, even to her, but it was the truth.

"What are you going to do about Gretchen's bills? I assume they are substantial."

Callie swallowed, then gritted her teeth as the movement ricocheted in her head. While she was careful not to share too much about her private life, Adam knew she had sole responsibility for her sister, who had Down Syndrome. "She's at Great Oaks."

She didn't say any more, didn't need to. His eyes telegraphed recognition. Great Oaks was one of the best and most expensive care communities in the DC area. To her mortification, tears welled up until he became little more than a watery blob.

That blob grabbed a tissue from the box beside the bed and leaned down, dabbing at her eyes. New tears rose to the surface at his gesture. She couldn't remember the last time someone had done something so sweet for her.

Note to self; get out more.

He dabbed some more. "You know, Cal, it wouldn't kill you to ask for help now and again."

Whoa. Was that the concussion speaking? Adam never got that personal. Not with her. "What?"

"Forget it." He straightened and tossed the tissue, basketball-style, into a tall trash can. "So…" Sighing, he focused on the wall behind her, just past her left ear. "You're telling me you spent your summer working full-time but only getting paid for half of it. And, you have no benefits?"

Well, when he put it that way… "Maybe."

He gave a hoarse laugh. "What are we going to do

about this?"

We? A jolt of hope struck her but, then again, she was heavily concussed. He might not mean anything by it.

Hopeful or hopeless, with her credit score, there was only one way forward and now was as good a time as any to take that step. "I had thought you could, you know…lend me some money. I'll pay you back."

Oh, Lord. Could she sound any more desperate?

At least, after all these weeks of worrying about it, it was out in the universe now. Holding her breath, she waited for his reaction, but he kept on staring at the damn wall.

Trying to find a polite excuse.

Double crap. She should have asked him to help her find a loan instead. His family rubbed elbows with lots of bigwigs in the banking business. That would have been more professional and much less awkward. Instead, she put her foot in it, as usual, grabbing at a solution better fit for a romance novel than real life.

Rising, he began to pace. "How much money are we talking about?" he asked, facing her from the end of the bed.

She swallowed. "I-I don't know, for sure. I hadn't gotten that far." Hadn't dreamed *they'd* get that far. Despite her throbbing brain, she did the math. "At least fifty thousand dollars." Needing to explain the large amount, she rushed on. "I need enough for Gretchen's health insurance, my insurance, and her rent. She gets a little something every month, but it isn't nearly enough. Great Oaks isn't the cheapest, but I'm not moving her. That's her home." Best to get that straight right off the bat. "Plus, she needs some new stuff that insurance won't pay for."

Callie had been trying for over a year to set money aside for an upgrade in OT and PT equipment, but at the rate that was going, it would take her forever.

"Look, it's a lot of money." Embarrassment stung her cheeks, and she waved the metaphorical white flag. "Let's forget about it. I-I don't know what I was thinking. I'm concussed, remember? If you could put a good word in at my bank..."

Shoving a hand through his hair, a habit he had when he was deep in thought, he began retracing his steps. "I may have a better idea."

Her stomach turned over again. "A better idea?" She didn't bother to hide her doubt. After all, she'd been trying to think of a better solution for the past six weeks and had come up completely empty-handed. Adam thought he'd found one in less than five minutes? He needed to think again. Getting a second job was impossible—when she wasn't at the university, she was with Gretchen. There was no other alternative. She had to have the money.

He returned to his spot on the bed, filling the hole left by his absence. "Something that benefits both of us. But it wouldn't be a loan. The money would be a...a gift."

Curiouser and curiouser. She lowered her eyes to his tie. Adam's ties were legendary throughout the university and the one anomaly to his sedate persona. They were loud, whimsical, and a complete paradox to his conservatively tailored suits. Today's tie, as was fitting for the first day of school, featured a cartoon of the university's bear mascot in all its feral glory.

Adorable.

One prime package.

Oh, for heaven's sake. The man isn't a piece of meat.

Drained, she fought another urge to lift her hand to her head. "Adam, I'm too tired to even pretend to know what you're talking about."

"It's simple, really." He gave her a pleased smile. "It solves all sorts of problems for both of us. In fact, I don't know why I haven't thought of it before. I think we should get married."

Despite the covers, Callie went from warm to ice cold. She clutched at the blanket with both hands, wadding it into a ball under her chin. "Oh, God. What aren't you telling me? Did they find a tumor? A brain bleed?"

His gaze narrowed. "What in the hell are you talking about?"

"I'm talking about my head. Obviously, there's something majorly wrong with it, because I thought I just heard you say we should get married." *Maybe a stroke. A stroke would do it.*

His symmetrical features relaxed into amusement again. "I get it. No, you aren't fatally ill, and yes, you did just hear me say that."

She forced herself to loosen her death grip on the blanket but still held onto it in case it was her last link to reality. "But you don't want to get married again. Ever." He must have said so a thousand times or more.

"True." He flashed his killer grin. "But this wouldn't be a real marriage. What I'm envisioning is more of a business arrangement. You'll help me convince the paparazzi that I'm no longer newsworthy, and I'll help you pay your bills. I can outline it all in a contract and everything, so there're no surprises."

Callie closed her eyes for a moment while her poleaxed brain tried to make sense of things. *A contract. No surprises.* At least that sounded more like the Adam she knew. But she still had lots of questions. And one Big Kahuna of a question.

She opened her eyes and met his head-on. "Why marriage?"

He slid off the bed again and walked to the window. He bent a metal slat in the mini-blind and peeked out at whatever view the room offered. "It's drastic, I know, but I think it's the only way to get the paparazzi off my back. We could pretend we were dating, but that would make it worse. They'd be all over both of us, waiting for one of us to cheat. Marriage has a nice, boring permanency about it. We give it two years, three years—however long it takes for my name to disappear from the gossip rags and for you to save some money, and then we quietly get a divorce." The metal blind snapped as he released it. Slipping his hands into his pants pockets, he returned to her side. "I really think it could work out well. For both of us."

She smoothed out the blanket, letting the waffle-like weave slide through her fingers. The whole idea was absurd. Drastic. And yet…

She met his eyes again. He'd said those three little magic words. *Save some money.* To have a nest egg. To not have to worry about paying Gretchen's bills. What would that feel like?

After years of living paycheck to paycheck, Callie wanted to find out.

"Okay. Count me in."

Chapter Two

"The hell you did!" Adam's older brother, John, slammed an elbow into Adam's solar plexus before pivoting and sinking a perfect three-pointer on the basketball court at their parents' sprawling Virginia farm.

"First...of all." Adam leaned over, forcing air into his lungs. "That...was a foul." He looked over at Mason through rivulets of sweat. "Did you...see that? Personal. Foul."

Mason raised a fisted hand to one eye and waggled it, as if wiping away imaginary tears. "There's no crying in basketball," he said, with the usual lack of brotherly sympathy. "Besides, I'm with Jeep on this one," he added, using John's longtime nickname, which had nothing to do with the car maker and everything to do with a childhood bastardization of his initials, "J" and "P".

"You honestly asked Callie to marry you?" Jeep caught the rebounding ball and circled back to where Adam stood, still hunched over and gasping for air. "And she honestly said 'yes'?"

Adam looked up at his brother, who possessed the same dark hair and deep blue eyes but was a more compact six-foot-three. What little he lacked in height, though, Jeep made up for in breadth. A former Navy SEAL with a chest-load of medals to prove it, Jeep still pursued the rigorous workouts of his younger years, despite his more sedentary current position as a JAG Corps lawyer.

"Yep. It's brilliant," Adam managed to gasp.

Jeep raised a skeptical eyebrow. "Oh, yeah? How so?"

Holding a hand to his tender midsection, Adam straightened and sucked in another deep breath. "It's like Mace said this morning—the press doesn't care diddly-squat for an old married couple. After I'm married, with any luck, I'll never see another paparazzo again."

"Sure," Mason said, joining them.

He topped Adam by an inch with the same rangy, muscular build. Years ago, his boyish good looks, blond hair, and blue eyes had modeling agencies knocking down his door, but medicine had been Mace's calling since childhood. He was one year into a grueling residency at a nearby hospital and one month into wedded bliss.

"It's great for you, but what does Callie get out of it? Aside from being chained to your sorry ass for the rest of her life," he added, cackling.

Adam shot Mason an intimidating look which only made his little brother laugh harder.

"I'm not a completely selfish prick," Adam began.

"No, not completely." Jeep stuck his fist out, and Mason bumped it with his own.

"Nice one," Mason said.

Adam ignored his brothers' juvenile behavior. "Callie isn't unhappy with the arrangement. I've promised her the money she needs to continue her sister's care, and I've worked up an agreement providing for Gretchen's support for five years after the termination of the marriage."

Mason groaned. "Man, listen to yourself! 'Termination of the marriage,' " he intoned in a robotic voice. "You really know how to sweep a girl off her feet."

"That's the whole point." Adam scowled. "This isn't a love match, Mace, it's a business arrangement. Callie knows that, and she's on board, one hundred percent."

Mason and Jeep exchanged loaded looks.

This time, Adam tried his work frown, the one that shot fear into the hearts of his students. Jeep grinned while Mason flipped Adam the bird.

"Thanks, asshole," he told his little brother. "Don't you guys get it? This solves things for both of us. It's a win-win."

"Huh." Jeep grunted while spinning the basketball on a finger. He watched the ball turn for a minute, then hugged it against his chest. "Here's the thing. We like Callie, and we don't want her hurt. She might be more vulnerable than you give her credit for—maybe not," he conceded, when Adam started to argue. "I don't know her very well, but what little I do know tells me she's been through a lot. Then there's you. Mallory's death." He shook his head. "A tragedy, plain and simple. But you deserve happiness, and we don't want you settling for less."

The mention of his wife's name knifed Adam's heart. He didn't want to talk about Mallory right now. Marriage to Callie—marriage to anyone—could never come close to the love and commitment he and Mal had shared. This was nothing more than what he'd said it was: a business deal.

"I'm happy enough. And I'm not settling. This is what I want." He snatched the ball away from Jeep and headed toward the basket.

"What was the response up at the house?" Mason asked, closing in on defense.

Adam pivoted, then ran straight into Jeep. Damn, his brothers had game. He blindly threw a couple of elbows and steamrolled toward the hoop.

"Haven't told them yet," he said, making a textbook lay-up.

Mason caught the bounce and hesitated, hands bracketing the ball. "I don't understand. Aren't you getting married *this* Saturday?"

"Yes."

Behind him, Jeep swore like the sailor he was.

"When are you planning on telling them? Your second anniversary?" He threw up his hands. "Man, you need to get your head out of your—"

Adam rolled his eyes. He was a grown man, for God's sake. "They'll know when they need to know."

"When who needs to know what, dearest?" The question, imbued with a crisp, formal British accent, came from behind the manicured boxwood hedge framing the paved court.

Their mother, her bobbed gray hair dotted with dried leaves, entered the court through the gap in the bushes. She carried a large basket over one arm.

"To get laid. That's what you *need*," Mason whispered to Adam. "Is that in your contract too?"

"Shut it, Mace." Adam emphasized his words by stepping on his brother's foot before moving over to his mother and peeking into her basket. "Hi, Mum. What are you collecting now?"

"Twigs," his mother answered, her blue gaze brimming with preoccupation. "For the next segment.

I'm making candleholders."

"Of course, you are." Chuckling, he dropped a kiss on her still-smooth cheek, a gesture Mason and Jeep copied in turn.

Adam had witnessed many people, upon their first meeting with Clementine "Minna" Mason Hughes, write her off as a total dingbat. It was a mistake they made only once. Born and raised in London, she'd met his father nearly forty years ago, while both attended Cambridge.

Upon her graduation—at the top of her class, no less—she'd gone on to create and star in a first-of-its-kind, do-it-yourself television show that tackled everything from flower arranging to plumbing. What began as thirty minutes on a local access channel had become a multi-billion-dollar food, craft, and home decorating empire.

And despite the countless demands on her time both within and without her own enterprise, Minna continued to host her own nationally syndicated DIY show. There was no task she couldn't master, including raising three rambunctious sons who thought she hung the moon.

"Candleholders, hmm?" Jeep winked at his brothers. "Won't the twigs catch fire?"

"You glue them to a glass jar, John dear, not to the candles themselves." Minna, who never used her eldest son's nickname, knelt before the shrubs. Without looking up, she waved a hand at her offspring. "Don't just stand there, boys. Start searching. Nothing larger than a quarter inch in diameter, please."

It never failed to amuse Adam that, regardless of how old he and his brothers got, his mother always referred to them collectively as "boys," and always roped them into her project *du jour*. Amid much laughter and teasing, they all began to, quite literally, pick up sticks.

Although he would never admit as much, Adam found such unscripted times with his family somewhat bittersweet. An only child, Mallory had adored the easy camaraderie and often outright craziness of his family. He, of course, had taken it all for granted until after Mallory's death, but since then, the poignant moments hit him hard. How Mal would have relished this hunt! The sight of the three Hughes "boys" searching on hands and knees for the right-sized twig would have had her laughing for days.

"Hey, Mum. Adam has some news."

Leaning back onto his heels, Adam glowered at Mason, who stuck his tongue out in response.

"Hmm. Good news, I hope?" Minna crawled under a boxwood after an elusive twig.

"Very good." Adam placed a hand on his mother's shoulder and helped untangle her from the bush without losing an eye in the process.

She stood and ran a hand through her hair, dislodging a flurry of debris. No one could accuse her of being afraid to get dirty. "Well, then! Do tell."

Jeep and Mason stopped their searches and stepped over to stand a few feet behind their mother, grinning like fools. The assholes were loving this.

Adam cleared his throat. "I had hoped to sit down with both you and Dad, but since the cat's out of the bag…" He glared at his brothers. "Callie and I are getting married."

In general, Minna Hughes was a grade-A professional when it came to covering her emotions. Anyone so consistently in the public eye learned not to bat an eyelash when things went a little sideways. But with family, her heart was stitched on her sleeve.

Her basket dropped unheeded to the ground as she embraced Adam, sweat and all, in a bone-crushing hug. "Oh, darling! How I've hoped and prayed...been so worried. It's lovely news. We didn't know you and Callie...I mean, we thought perhaps Angela...but it's simply lovely."

He caught about eighty percent of the words she blubbered into his shoulder. Patting her on the back, he mouthed, "This is all your fault," to his brothers. To his mother, he said, "Sorry to throw it at you like that. I wanted to wait and tell you after we'd gotten—"

"Don't you dare tell me I'm not invited to this wedding!" Minna swatted at his chest, her fist full of twigs. "Your younger brother has already played the elopement card, thank you very much."

With horror, Adam recognized the gleam in his mother's eyes and raised his hands. "Hang on, Mum. We don't want any fuss. It's not that kind of wed—"

"Nonsense. If you won't do it for yourself, think of Callie. Such a nice girl, and she handles you so well. I'm certain you'll be very happy together. Now, let me think." She glanced around at the wide expanse of yard, bordered by her well-loved gardens and the glistening Potomac below. "For a fall wedding, we'll need warm colors."

"No, Mum, seriously, we don't want anything." Panic made him sound breathy. "And what do you mean, she handles me well?"

Mason and Jeep doubled over.

"She means, Callie doesn't take any of your sh—"

"Shenanigans," Mason cut off Jeep's more colorful word.

Minna had a strict zero tolerance policy when it came to swearing. Since Adam and his brothers had reached adulthood, her swear jar donations were, at a minimum, one hundred bucks a word. For years, they'd made a game out of substituting benign words for the more colorful ones.

"Right." Jeep tossed Mason a grateful look. "You're more yourself when you're around her."

Adam frowned. "I'm always myself."

"Sorry, bro," Mason said. "Not true. You may not see it, but you've gotten pretty good at freezing people out over the past few years. When you're with Callie, you thaw out a little."

Adam huffed at this psychoanalysis. All he'd wanted to do tonight was play the standing Tuesday night game of hoops with his brothers, followed by a relaxed family dinner. He'd only mentioned his arrangement with Callie to Mason and Jeep because he was so pleased with it.

In hindsight, Adam should have known his brothers wouldn't be able to keep their mouths shut. He and Callie had agreed to act first and apologize later. However, now that his mother had her garden-gloved hands in the works, all bets were off.

"We must tell your grandfather right away," Minna said, retrieving her basket and resuming her twig search on hands and knees. "He'll be delighted, but we need to let his security detail know ASAP so they can arrange things. They never like last-minute plans." Her laughter was muffled by the bush she reached into. "For that matter, neither does your father."

At the mention of the Secret Service entourage, Adam gave it one more try. "Honestly, we hadn't planned on anything big. We can slip away on Saturday and keep it simple."

"Saturday!"

His mother whipped around so fast, Adam was surprised she didn't break in two.

"But that's less than a week away."

"I know, but there was an incident today at the university. Callie wound up in the hospital with a concussion and that…changed things."

"Oh, dear. She'll be all right?" At his nod, his mother set her basket aside and pursed her lips. "Hmmm. She'll need something nice and cheery while she's recovering. It's a tricky time of the year for fresh flowers, but I'll check the greenhouse and see what's still blooming."

"That would be nice." Adam said, although he didn't give a rat's ass about flowers. He had to get his mother to back off the romance. "When I saw her at the hospital, it brought up some things."

"And all at once, you knew she was the one!"

Out of respect, he squelched an eye roll. So much for losing the romance. When his mother got going, there was no stopping her.

"That's how it was with your father and me. Have I ever told you about the bonfire and—"

"Yes, you have," Adam and his brothers confirmed in unison.

Her mouth slipped into a stubborn pout, and she set her garden-gloved hands on her hips. "Fine. But surely you want your father to perform the ceremony? Why don't we plan on having something intimate here?" She waved a hand, encompassing the pretty red-brick, white-trimmed colonial house and the surrounding acreage.

The fight fizzled out of Adam like air from a popped balloon. With one last, I'm-gonna-kill-you look at his brothers, he nodded. "Okay, Mum. If Callie's up for it, that sounds great."

****

"Wakey, wakey, eggs and bakey," Callie sang out as she prodded the lump in the bed clothes.

"Callie!" Gretchen's muffled voice hailed from somewhere under the mound of blankets—all of them sporting a rainbow, a unicorn, or both—covering her bed.

"Present! Present! Present!" She shouted excitedly, pushing out from under the covers. With a laugh, she blew at the wayward strands of dark blonde hair that fell over her light brown eyes.

Callie joined in the laughter and pushed Gretchen's tangled hair behind her sister's ear, which wasn't easy considering the moving target. "No present today. It's not your birthday anymore, remember? That was last week."

Gretchen fished a large, stuffed unicorn out from under the bedclothes and hugged it tightly. "I love my new unicorn, Cal." She gave her big sister a noisy kiss on the cheek.

Callie smiled. There was one thing she could always count on: no matter how upset or worried she was, visiting Gretchen made the day better. Nothing got her sister down. She loved her life at Great Oaks and her part-time job in a nearby library.

If marriage to Adam meant keeping her sister's world unchanged, Callie was all in. Speaking of him, he was going to raise holy hell after he found out she'd checked herself out of the hospital early, but she'd promised her sister she'd stop by tonight, and a promise to Gretchen was a promise kept.

"I'm glad you like it. Did you have a nice nap?"

Frowning, Gretchen ignored the question and pointed to Callie's head instead. "What happened?"

Callie raised a hand to the bandage taped to a shaved patch above her left ear. A glimpse of herself in a hospital mirror had confirmed the worst. She already had a permanent chin-to-nose scar that made her look like the Bride of Frankenstein. Now, with the new injury… Well, it wasn't fair.

"Um, yeah. It's nothing. Just a bump on the head." That was still thumping like a tune from one of their father's old jazz recordings, but she'd live.

Gretchen leaned closer. "Your eye looks funny."

That would be the shiner. Callie had done her best with the makeup she had in her bag, but it wasn't enough to fool anyone, and Gretchen on a bad day was more observant than Sherlock Holmes on a good one.

"Wanna hold Betty?" Gretchen held up her new unicorn and tears stung Callie's eyes.

The offer was typical of her little sister—empathetic to the core—but that wasn't what caused the tears. Every one of her sister's many stuffed animals were named "Betty," after their mother. Callie had given up on sentimentality a long time ago, but it surprised her every time her sister used the familiar name.

Callie patted the animal's glittery pink horn. "Thanks for offering, but I'm okay." She smiled, knowing the impact her next words would have. "I have a surprise for you."

Gretchen's brown eyes sparkled, and she threw the unicorn up in the air, unfazed when it landed on the floor beside the bed. "What is it? Tell me. Tell me!"

"I will, if you'll stop wiggling," Callie said, with another laugh.

At this ultimatum, Gretchen froze mid-movement. She loved surprises above all else the world had to offer, apart from unicorns, and she wouldn't risk one for anything.

"Ready?"

Gretchen gave the scantest of nods.

Callie took a deep breath. "I'm getting married."

"Ooooh!" Gretchen's wiggles returned with a vengeance.

Leaping from the bed, she ran over to her dresser where more unicorns, of various shapes and sizes, sat in a row. With an excited squeak, she grabbed one decked out in full bridal regalia, right down to the ridiculously long white veil sewn to its horn.

For the first time since the attack, Callie managed a real smile. Weddings were a big deal to her sister. They closed out all her favorite movies.

"You're gonna wear a dress like this?" Gretchen's awe was palpable as she reverently stroked the white satin skirt hiding the unicorn's hind legs.

Callie's smile faded. Damn. Why hadn't she thought of it before? Gretchen would expect this wedding to have all the trimmings. "Um. Maybe, maybe not." That was fifty percent true.

Gretchen set the stuffed animal on Callie's shoulder and gently draped the veil over Callie's face. "There." She sat back and admired her handiwork. "You look pretty, Callie."

Callie gave a strangled laugh, unsure of what to say. Of course, she looked better. The gauzy lace covered her

31

scarred and bruised face.

"Thanks." Shrugging, she removed the veil and returned the toy.

"Who's your prince?" Gretchen asked, making the unicorn gallop up and down the mountain range of blankets covering her bed.

"My what?"

"Who are you gonna marry?"

"Oh, right. I'm marrying Adam, the man I work for." The words prompted more than a few tingles in naughty places.

No. She cut off the direction of her thoughts. There would be no lusting in this marriage. She'd banned that kind of thinking at work, so it shouldn't be too hard to keep it out of her private time.

Except that she was marrying Adam Hughes. *Holy crap, Batman.*

This whole day resembled a dream—both the blissful and *bete noir* varieties. For the umpteenth time since the attack, anxiety expanded in her throat. What if this was some weird, concussion-induced fantasy world she'd been dropped into? Just in case, she pinched herself. Hard.

She rubbed at the sore, pink mark on her arm. *Nope, not a dream.* For the umpteenth-plus-one time today, she wasn't certain how that made her feel.

Gretchen, lips pursed in concentration, paused as her unicorn reached a woolen precipice. "Adam's not a prince. He writes books. But not *that* kind of book."

Callie hid a grin. This was Gretchen's standard response whenever Adam's name came up. One day, she'd returned from an outing to find Callie waiting for her, reading one of his books. When Gretchen had begged to have the story read aloud, Callie had replied it wasn't "*that* kind of book," and the tagline had stuck.

"But I guess it's okay because you love him," Gretchen stated matter-of-factly before resuming her play. "Can we go get some ice cream, please?"

After this verbal bombshell, however, Callie wasn't ready to move on to a sugar high. "Wait. What makes you think I'm in love with Adam?"

Giggling, Gretchen turned to look at her. "Because your eyes smile whenever you talk about him, silly."

Sighing, Callie stretched out on the bed, keeping her weight on her elbows to protect her head. Son of a gun. Her eyes "smiled," did they? *That* would have to stop. Like right now.

God, she hoped no one else had noticed.

Especially not her "prince."

Chapter Three

Pounding.

Slowly, the layers of fog around Callie's brain were pierced by fierce, staccato pounding.

"What the...?" She bolted upright, instantly regretting the move. Now there was pounding both inside and outside her head.

"Coming," she grumbled, in the general direction of the external noise.

She cast her un-swollen eye toward the green, digital clock display on her microwave. 11:02. So, it only felt like the middle of the night. She must have fallen asleep right after she got home from Gretchen's. Not that it mattered. In Callie's small studio apartment, the sofa pulled double duty as her bed.

She took the obligatory moment to massage her hip, which was no fan of sleeping on the couch, before hobbling over and flipping on the overhead florescent. The sudden transition from night to day left her blinking. The harshness of the ugly fluorescent fixture was filtered by an old, pink sheet she'd attached to the even uglier ceiling tiles, but it was still stark enough when one was both half-awake and wholly concussed.

Another round of sharp raps on the door reminded her why she was upright. "Okay, okay. Keep your pants on." She put her good eye to the peephole.

And saw the last person she'd ever expected to see outside her apartment door.

With a haste that made her all thumbs, she unbolted the two heavy-duty deadbolts she'd insisted her landlord install, given the ridiculously crappy part of DC in which she lived.

"Adam!" She threw the door wide. "What are you doing here?"

Scowling, he pushed past her and stood, hands on hips, looking as out of place in her living-room-cum-kitchen-cum-bedroom as a cow in a henhouse. He surveyed her home sweet home in seconds before aiming his steely blue gaze in her direction.

Uh-oh. She recognized that look. Furious was an understatement. He was flat-out livid.

"Grab your stuff. I want you out of this neighborhood now."

Her hackles rose automatically at his masterful tone, and she took her time re-locking the door in an effort to keep her temper in check.

"Look, *Dr. Hughes.*" She purposely used the formal address, knowing it irked him. *Passive-aggressive R us.* "It may not be the Ritz, but it's clean, affordable, and cozy." Lifting her chin, she met his eyes with her haughtiest look. "I'm proud of it."

She was. It smelled as nice as dollar-store vanilla candles could make it and featured an eye-popping color scheme. Her childhood had been spent in a colorless, unloved house of beiges and browns, so she'd put a lot of effort into making this room as cheery as possible.

She'd broken the landlord's rules and repainted the dingy walls a soft sunset pink and filled the room with as many pink, orange, and yellow throw pillows as she could sew and knit. The threadbare couch was swathed in a multicolored blanket her grandmother had crocheted sometime during the 1970s, and Callie loved every colorful inch.

And, of course, there were plants. Everywhere. She collected foliage the way spinsters collected cats—most of them rescued from the dumpster. There was something wonderfully uplifting in bringing something, even a plant, back from the brink.

No, the apartment wasn't much, but she liked to think she'd made the most of it.

Raking a hand through his hair, Adam walked over and examined the giant yellow-brown water stain covering the wall above her sink.

She rolled her eyes, then wished she hadn't as her temple pulsed again. It figured he would zoom in on the one thing that had withstood years of scrubbing and several coats of paint. "Let's leave Walter out of this."

Adam gave her an over-the-shoulder glance before returning to his study of the wall again. "Walter?"

She took a couple of uneven steps toward him and gestured toward the wall. "The stain. It keeps coming back, no matter what I try, so I named it 'Walter.' I think it looks like a turtle. I tried to cover it up with a poster, but nothing sticks there."

Dear God. Talk about verbal diarrhea. Oh, well. He probably wasn't all that surprised. She'd named her computer and printer at work too—Bonnie and Clyde. Bonnie was the computer and the brains of the outfit while Clyde, the laser printer, couldn't always be trusted. Besides, if Adam was committed to this crazy marriage plan, it was important he understand what he was getting into.

His head tilted this way and that as he re-examined the splotch on the wall. Then, muttering something that sounded suspiciously four-lettered—rare for him—he faced her again. He'd exchanged his more formal school clothes for jeans and a threadbare T-shirt that bore his grandfather's campaign slogan from three elections ago: *Let's Heal with Hughes.*

Impaired vision or no, Callie admired the way the well-washed fabric clung to his wide shoulders and the chiseled contours of his chest and abdomen. The man was a workaholic. When did he find the time to work out? The evenings, apparently. The damp, dark waves of his hair were tousled from his hand's recent foray, and he smelled of soap.

Adam in a business suit? Sexy as hell. Adam in casual clothes?

There were no words.

But it was obvious he was still boiling mad. The scant three feet separating them shimmered with the heat of his barely controlled anger. "Believe it or not *Ms. Wallis*, I am not here to pass judgment on your apartment."

Liar. Liar. Disapproval was written all over his face, in flashing neon lights.

"I am here because you checked yourself out of the hospital. Prematurely. So, I repeat, grab your stuff. We're going to my apartment, where I can keep an eye on you."

She stood her ground. "There's no need for any of that, Adam. I don't need a nursemaid. I've got a bump on my head. Fine. I'm dealing with it." Albeit not very well, since she was supposed to have changed her bandage by now. "Besides, it was costing a fortune, and I had to visit Gretchen. No big deal."

His features softened a fraction. "I'm not mad at

you, Callie. I'm mad at myself. I should have known, long before now, where you lived. I should have… No, look." He raised his hand when she opened her mouth. "I applaud the effort you've put into this place. I was raised by the Queen of DIY, and I recognize your hard work. But no amount of paint will move this apartment into a safe part of town. I can't believe you haven't been mugged or worse while living here."

She stared down at the frayed hole in the corner of her thrifted rug, weighing whether to come clean. The worst was out. He knew where she lived. Plus, one of the few pieces of advice her mother had passed on was that it was better to tell the truth than be caught in a lie. As a rule, Callie followed that advice, save one exception. One doozy of an exception.

But this wasn't it. Sighing, she met his stormy blues. "I was mugged once, when I first moved in, right before I began working for you. *But…*" She scanned his face for signs of more softening. No such luck. "I learned my lesson. Since then, I've been extremely careful." She had to be. A woman with her iffy balance was always at a physical disadvantage, even in the best of times. "I have a system."

A muscle jumped in his jaw. "A system?"

Honestly, he needed to stop clenching his beautiful teeth. He was going to chip one.

"Yes. Paul's the landlord. He's lived here forever, and he's a big man. A *huge* man. He's got a reputation—something about selling drugs—but to me, he's a total kitty cat."

Adam shoved his hands into his jeans pockets, possibly to keep from throttling her, but he remained silent while she continued. "For a small price, Pauly walks me to the Metro station every morning and escorts me home every night. If he can't go, one of his sons fills in. He and his wife have six sons and they're all known as, um, bad asses."

Adam folded his arms across his broad chest. "A family-man drug dealer?" He cocked an eyebrow. "Really? Just what, may I ask, is the price for this protection service?"

Her face flamed but she continued to keep his gaze. "Every week I bake them a triple batch of my grandmother's chocolate-chip cookies. Unless it's Christmastime. Then I make your mom's frosted sugar cookies. Pauly has a mouth full of sweet teeth."

She half held her breath, unsure of what his response might be to this confession. It sounded ridiculous, but the arrangement had worked well for years, and she wasn't going to apologize for it. "Desperate times and all that," she added. Fact was her cookies were *that* good.

If possible, Adam's eyes grew even darker. From habit ingrained in childhood, she tensed, bracing herself for a verbal attack.

Instead, he burst out laughing. Erupted was more accurate, into a belly laugh of a magnitude she had never witnessed from the indomitable Adam Hughes. On the Richter scale of laughs, this one was a ten.

It was also infectious. She began laughing and kept at it until her head hurt so much, she had to stop. Probing her bandage, making certain it hadn't slipped, she sobered as best she could, entranced by the merriment shining in his eyes. Never, at any time in the past five years, had he been so animated, so free from the shadows of the past.

It propelled her forward, like a strange, cosmic force

pushing at her backside. Her heart pounded in her chest while saliva pooled in her mouth.

Holiest of crap! Every day, ordinary, taciturn Adam was a ten on the hotness scale, but this unrestrained version broke the damn scale.

Then, poof! In seconds, the old familiar coolness displaced the warmth.

Damn it.

She missed what she'd glimpsed. Not that he was as icy with her as he was with people in general; thankfully, that layer had thawed several years ago. But that laughter. Wow. Would there be more of that warmth and trust once they were married?

She hoped so but feared not.

"Seriously, Callie. Go get..." The corners of his mouth twitched. "Let me rephrase that. Would you please consider coming over to my place? It would make me feel a whole lot better." He ran a hand through his hair again. "It's been one helluva day, and I don't know about you, but I'm still reeling over the fact you were attacked. At the risk of sounding like a Neanderthal, I will sleep better knowing you're not alone." He cast a doubtful look at her couch. "I have a very nice guest room that becomes yours on Saturday anyway. Look at it as an early move-in date."

She retracted her hackles. When he put it that way, she couldn't argue. Didn't want to argue. Truth was, he had her at sleeping in a real bed. "Okay. But as we agreed, I'm keeping my apartment."

His mouth flattened as he took another glance around the tiny room, ending with the ancient front door. "I'm fine with you keeping your own place, but why don't you let me pay for—"

"Nope. I'm paying, which means I keep this place in all its glory, or the deal's off."

After a long beat, he extended his hand. "Okay. Deal. But I'm buying you a new lock. Or four."

She slipped her hand against his and shook. His hand was warm, his grasp firm, but he didn't crush her hand the way some men did. The brief contact set her nerve endings jangling with the same hard-core, animal attraction she'd fought against every day for the past five years.

God help her. Today, she'd agreed to marry him, to live with him, for the next two years, with an open option for more.

It would be pure heaven…and total hell.

She looked forward to every second of it.

****

The last time Adam had worn so many layers of clothes at breakfast was when he was three. Not that he was wearing that much—a pair of joggers, a T-shirt, and his tired Georgetown sweatshirt weren't exactly overkill. However, considering his usual routine involved wolfing down a piece of peanut butter toast while standing at the sink in his boxers, he felt overdressed today.

He'd also had a go at making a real breakfast after—wonders never ceased—setting two spots at the breakfast bar. Of course, his mother had made sure her sons were no strangers to a kitchen, but his culinary skills had evaporated after Mallory's death. Today, as he threw eggs, cheese, and veggies into a frozen pie crust, he discovered he missed cooking. In particular, he missed cooking for someone else.

"Oh!"

He looked up from plating the hot quiche to see

Callie hovering at the edge of the kitchen. Her good eye was wide open, and she stared at the kitchen floor as if she expected the final step into the room might bite.

Her bad eye looked like she'd been in a prizefight and lost. Adam held back a two-hundred-dollar swear word and pasted on a smile. "Just in time. I hope you like quiche."

"I-I…" She swallowed and shrugged. "Um, sure. That's fine. I didn't expect…You didn't have to make anything. I'm good with toast."

He gave her what he hoped was an encouraging smile that deepened when she walked over to the bar. She braced a hand on the counter, blinking sleepily at his black leather and chrome bar stools. Most of her thick, blonde hair had escaped its braid, but the gauze bandage above her ear didn't appear to have slipped any during the night. A red line, a fraction above the faint scar on her cheek, revealed where her head had rested against the pillow.

Difficult to believe, but he couldn't remember her hair ever being out of its usual scrunchy up-do before. Corkscrew curly, it hung almost to her waist. Glorious. Then his drifting gaze came to a screeching halt at her toes. Her neon-pink painted toes. Sweet heaven. It had been a long time since a woman's bare feet had crossed his kitchen floor.

Even with the bandage and the black eye, she looked super sexy.

Wait. What? That wasn't right. He must be hungry or need more caffeine because this was *Callie*. Sure, she was attractive, in a girl-next-door way, but physical attraction wasn't part of their relationship. Never had been, never would be. Period.

"Would you mind if I stood?" Pink flooded her cheeks as she continued to stare at the modern bar stools.

"No, I..." Good Lord. He was such an idiot! The stools.

It would be difficult for her to climb onto one with her injured hip. She didn't baby it, but the stools were tall. Within seconds, he'd detoured toward the kitchen table. The sunny window made the eating nook cozy and intimate, so he'd chosen the more remote-feeling bar. He should have remembered.

"Oh, no, please don't move everything for me." Her gaze dropped, calling attention to her incredible lashes— dark, naturally thick, devoid of makeup.

That was one of the things he appreciated about Callie. Unlike most of the females he rubbed elbows with, even his beloved Mallory, she kept her makeup to the bare minimum. Unless his eyes fooled him, she only wore a little lip gloss on those full, luscious pink lips.

Shit. He plunked their plates down with more force than necessary and turned away to retrieve their place settings. She'd spent one night in his apartment and here he was, awkward as a schoolboy. For this arrangement to work, he had to remain as businesslike around her at home as he did at the office. Maybe more so, given the intimacy of sharing personal space.

Act cool. He could do that. Was good at it, even.

Pushing the plates as far from each other as the round white table permitted, he set down forks, knives, and paper napkins before waving her into one of the chairs. "I'm sorry about the bar...I didn't think."

She took a seat, her attention focused on the sunny window and the busy Georgetown traffic three stories below. "It's okay." Her voice was soft, her swallow audible.

Double-shit. He'd hurt her feelings. She'd made it clear a long time ago that her scar and hip, as well as the accident that caused them, were taboo subjects. He didn't know why he was having so much trouble finding his footing this morning.

He cleared his throat. Coffee. That would right the ship. He busied himself at the machine, relishing the simple routine.

"What do you think of the apartment?" He didn't try to disguise the pride of ownership in his voice.

After Mallory's death, he'd sold the sprawling Virginia house they'd shared and become a dedicated urbanite. This was one of the most sought-after buildings in the city, and his penthouse was the best of the best.

"Hmm." Callie looked around. "It's um…very white."

He raised his eyebrows. Typically, his apartment and decor received rave reviews from the handful of people invited to see it. He'd hired a very trendy, very *expensive* New York City decorator to make the place one hundred and eighty degrees from the cozy farmhouse he and Mallory had shared.

The decor was ultra-modern—white, with flashes of black here and there, mixed with the bright gleam of chrome—and exactly what he'd wanted: Clean. Functional. Sedate.

He flashed back to the colorful closet Callie called an apartment and chuckled. No wonder she was overwhelmed by the white. "I must admit, it's the polar opposite of your place."

Her shoulders relaxed as she ran a finger along the arm of the clear acrylic chair in which she sat. "Polar, as in polar bear. It's all black and white."

She gave a husky little laugh, and his gut clenched. Seriously, what was he, twelve? He had to get a grip.

"But it's very well done," she added, her eyes apologetic. "Like something out of a magazine. Did your mother help you?"

He exchanged the full cup of coffee at the coffee maker for an empty one before inserting another pod and pushing the brew button again.

"Nope." He set the steaming mug down beside her, along with a small pitcher. They'd worked together long enough for him to know she liked her coffee with lots of cream. "Mum isn't overly fond of it. In fact, she's been threatening to sneak in here and toss a few orange throw pillows on the couch when I'm not looking."

Now Callie gave him a genuine laugh, head back, pale length of her throat exposed, the morning light bringing out the red glints in her curly hair. "You're speaking my language. As you now know, color is my style. But this is your home. I want to bring a few things from my place, but I'll try and keep my crazy rainbow relegated to the guest room."

He carried the second cup of coffee over and took his place across from her. She'd voiced her comments with good humor, but this arrangement wasn't a dictatorship. Not that Callie could be dictated to. Her obstinate spunk was one of the many things about her that he appreciated. Except when it drove her to check herself out of a hospital with a head injury.

Leaning forward, he tapped the tabletop with his fingertips. "Callie, I want you to feel at home here. You're welcome to change whatever you wish."

Despite the words, fear twisted in his gut. Change.

That wasn't his forte. But he stood by what he'd said. The only way this would work was if they both made concessions. Shaking off his unease, he picked up his fork.

"Dig in," he invited and took a bite.

She followed suit. "Mmmm. Delicious." Another flush filled her cheeks as she eyed the dirty dishes by the sink. "Wait. You made this yourself?"

He forked another mouthful. "Yep. Mum's recipe, of course. Don't tell her I didn't make the crust." The outright shock on her face made him laugh. "It's only a quiche, Cal. Not rocket science."

"I beg to differ. I can bake cookies until the cows come home. Flour, sugar, butter, and eggs. It never changes. But actual meals? No way. That's wizardry." She waved her fork over her plate, "I still say you shouldn't have gone to the trouble, but my taste buds are glad you did."

With something close to horror, he realized he was the one blushing now. How sad that he'd grown so awkward when it came to doing something nice for someone other than himself. Callie had stuck with him through good and bad. She deserved a hell of a lot more than a quiche.

At the very least, say "thank you" more often, A-hole.

He cleared his throat again, dislodging the guilt. "So, how's the head? Bandage looks okay."

She wrinkled her nose. "It's fine. Sore, but fine. Although, I still can't remember what happened."

"I can tell you what little I know." He'd avoided the subject last night, but she deserved transparency now. "I've spoken to both the campus police and Ron, who sends you his best, by the way. The hallway video shows a man in a hoodie sitting on the bench outside the office. He keeps his face hidden behind a big pair of sunglasses the whole time. He follows you into the office, closes the door, and exits just shy of three minutes later. A few minutes after that, a passing student notices you lying on the floor of the office, gets Ron, and all hell breaks loose. Campus police, fire department, paramedics—you name them, they showed up. Is this ringing any bells?"

Frowning, she moved her head a mere fraction of an inch to the left, then stopped, no doubt so she didn't stir up a headache. He'd only had one concussion in his life, but he remembered the pain.

"No, and it's frustrating the hell out of me. I remember speaking to Ron before I climbed the stairs to the office. I want to say I talked to someone up there, too, but I'm not sure about that. I guess I opened the office door..." She rubbed her forehead, as if the touch would help summon the memories, and met his gaze with her own questioning one. "You said that's where they found me, but I don't have any memory of it. Is anything missing?"

"You mean besides a chunk of your head?" He gave her a sympathetic smile. "I can't tell yet. The office was pretty well worked over. I straightened up as best I could, but it will take your magic powers to really set things right."

He saluted her with his mug. Callie was a meticulous organizer, repurposing old metal baskets, tins, and other upcycled finds into genius storage hacks that were both useful and chic. It had become a good-natured source of teasing between them.

Since she could find things before he needed them,

he didn't object to her storing envelopes in an old metal lunch box or keeping his periodicals corralled in a former high school locker. In fact, although he'd never said as much, he found it sort of welcoming—like stepping back in time. Not an uncomfortable feeling for a professor of history.

He took a few more sips, savoring the taste of the rich Hawaiian coffee he loved while his mind circled back to the break-in. "It doesn't make any sense. I don't keep anything of real value at school. All my exams are on my notebook." He gestured toward the counter, where his computer rested securely in his black shoulder bag. "All the Bridges books are on my other computer, which I never bring to the office. But our friend in the hoodie was looking for something. Every book in the office was knocked off the shelves." He blew out a breath. "I just don't get it."

She finished the last of her breakfast and cradled her coffee mug with both hands, as if warming her fingers. "I agree. It makes no sense at all. Maybe they had the wrong office? Although I can't think of anyone who keeps anything of real value at school. Every other week Security comes out with a memo warning against it."

He nodded. "Well, they've upped the number of guards in the building and are looking at additional video, trying to get some idea of who and why." He took another long sip and sat back. "In the meantime, you are officially off-duty for the rest of the week."

She looked ready to protest, so he raised a hand. "I insist. Also…" He gathered courage for the next subject on his agenda. "You'll probably—make that definitely—be getting a call from my mother. I shared our plans with my family, and they are insisting we have a small ceremony out at my parents' place."

Callie winced. "I was afraid of that." She let out a heavy sigh. "Gretchen is all gung-ho about the wedding too. She's even expecting a wedding dress."

The memory of Mallory, radiant in her designer wedding gown, smiling up at him through her veil while slipping her hand into his, raced through his mind. This was exactly why he hadn't wanted any fuss. This marriage was as different from his first as night was from day. The ceremony should reflect that.

"I guess it wouldn't hurt, would it? I mean, to do something simple, so everyone feels included? I promise I won't get overtly bridal or anything."

Every fiber of his being screamed in protest, but he remembered what his brothers had said about not hurting her feelings. He didn't want to come across as a total prick. "All right. But I still say the simpler the better."

Stress lines formed between Callie's brows. "Simple." She dumped more cream into her already tan coffee and stirred. "You haven't met my sister yet. But I'll do my best."

That was all he could ask for or expect.

Chapter Four

Callie stood in front of the long mirror, twisting this way and that, as a mix of adrenaline and three cups of coffee wreaked havoc with her heart rate. Fifteen minutes until the ceremony and she hadn't chickened out. Yet. Even more impressive, she'd managed to get dressed without staining, tearing, or otherwise harming her dress. If she said so herself, she looked good.

She'd combed every vintage clothing store in the DC metro area, searching for the right mix of simplicity, elegance and, for Gretchen's sake, romance. As soon as Callie had spotted it on the rack, she'd fallen in love with the rose-pink midi dress, with its satin shoulder straps and gauzy, empire styling.

Now, after a few adjustments on her grandmother's ancient sewing machine and several late nights' worth of embroidery, she was happy with the effect. The graceful fall of the skirt hid the unevenness of her hips without adding bulk, while the decorative stitches along the modest neckline added the necessary romantic touch.

The bedroom door flew open, banging like a drum as it hit the doorstop. "Good God, Gretchen!" Callie pressed a hand to her chest. "You nearly gave me a heart attack."

Gretchen ignored the words and gave Callie a long, exuberant hug. Callie returned it, then stepped away, casting a critical eye down her sister's cobalt blue dress. Another vintage find, it had also spent some time at the sewing machine and within the embroidery hoop. The result was a dress that paired nicely with Callie's without being too similar or, much to Gretchen's dismay, too over-the-top.

"Eloise and I rode in a big black car," Gretchen said, looking around the room with great interest. "Is this your new house?"

"No, it belongs to Adam's mom and dad." They had insisted Callie use one of their guest bedrooms to dress.

The beautiful room, filled with the homey, antique accents Callie preferred over the cold, hard lines of Adam's apartment, only added to her general sense of having fallen into an alternate universe.

"Where *is* Eloise?" she asked, hoping to sidetrack her sister before Gretchen dove too deeply into the subject of living arrangements, bedrooms in particular.

Since the DC area was crowded and difficult to navigate, whenever Gretchen traveled without a family member, she was accompanied by a caregiver. Lately, that role had been filled by Eloise Snow, a sweet, shy nursing student whom both Gretchen and Callie liked.

"Potty. When are you going to put on your veil?" Gretchen ran a careful hand over the vintage tulle-and-lace garment. She'd made it clear it was her favorite part of Callie's outfit.

"Remember, it's not a veil. I mean, it used to be a veil, but I've turned it into a scarf." She lifted the ethereal piece, dyed to match her dress and trimmed with handmade velvet flowers.

It floated, soft as a feather, around her neck, with one length trailing along the front while the other flowed down her back. Very Audrey Hepburn, she hoped. An unorthodox look for a bride perhaps, but it was in line with Callie's love for upcycled couture. As a bonus, it fulfilled her sister's demand that there be a veil, without appearing too bridal.

"Oooh!" Gretchen squealed in delight. "You look beautiful, Cal!"

Callie turned a critical eye to the mirror once more. Beautiful, never. Not her. The puckered scar was still there, like a beacon, marring one side of her face. An army of butterflies went medieval in her stomach as she zeroed in on the scarf. A bride. Now, she looked like a bride.

Damn it. She'd promised she wouldn't. Would it terrify Adam? It kinda terrified her. Strange, but she'd assumed she'd never get married. As in never ever. But thanks to budget cuts and the out-of-control paparazzi, there she was.

She blew out a breath. To hell with second and third thoughts. This was happening—had to happen. Crossing to the large, four-poster bed, she picked up a shoe box bearing the name of an expensive designer across its lid. Time for the final touch. Clutching the box almost furtively, she carried it over to the mirror and removed the lid.

There they were. Nestled within fancy gold tissue paper sat the most gorgeous and ridiculously expensive pair of shoes she had ever owned. They weren't the four-inch heels she'd dreamed of wearing in her youth. Thanks to the accident, those were now a physical impossibility.

However, these shoes were a fabulous second-place prize. A mix of pink satin and exquisite, multi-colored beadwork, the flats kicked the "wow" factor of her outfit up four notches.

"Fairy shoes!" Gretchen looked at the size nine beauties with awe.

Callie gave her a big smile. "Exactly." Sinking onto the nearby chair, she slid them on.

Dear Lord. It must be a sin to love a pair of shoes so much, but if this damned her for eternity? Totally. Worth. It. Shoving herself upright again, she took a few slow steps. *Atta girl.* Pain or no, she refused to limp down the aisle.

She hadn't worked this hard on her gait since those endless months of physical therapy years ago. If she chose to pretend five days of sleeping on a real mattress hadn't helped her hip, that was her business.

A soft knock sounded at the door.

"Come on in, El," Callie said, without turning around.

"It's just me. I don't mean to bother, but I wanted— Oh, Callie! How beautiful you look!" Minna Hughes entered the room, her arms overflowing with a riot of perky blooms that defied the season. "And those shoes!" She nodded. "Gorgeous and simply divine with that dress." She turned to Gretchen with a smile and unloaded half the flowers she held. "Both you and your big sister look like princesses, my dear."

Gretchen giggled and buried her nose in a ginormous peony. The night before, Adam's parents had insisted that Callie and her sister join their family for a rehearsal dinner. Protective of Gretchen since the day of her birth, Callie had worried about her sister's acceptance, but her fears had been groundless.

The entire clan, including patriarch and former president John Patrick Hughes, had welcomed Gretchen to the family with open arms. In fact, their warmth and sincerity hit Callie so hard, it nearly sent her packing. She had little experience with such an outpouring of kindness. That it had come from the family to whom she owed so much—more than they would ever know—was more than a tad overwhelming.

"Thank you so much, Minna." The intimate form of address sounded foreign on Callie's tongue as she accepted her own bouquet, but the older woman had insisted they were now on a first-name basis. "These flowers are amazing. I can't believe you found such variety in the middle of September."

Minna gestured toward the wide expanse of windows in the far wall. "They're from the greenhouses. I put most of my efforts into vegetables, but I can't help keeping a few flowering plants. A fresh posy or two in the dead of winter does wonders for the spirit."

Before Callie could wrap her head around the concept of having not just one but multiple greenhouses at one's disposal, Minna took a full turn around her, humming with approval.

"I must say, your dress is exactly right. You've done a wonderful job." Only the faintest of wrinkles formed around the older woman's eyes when she smiled. "Careful, my dear, or you'll find yourself on television, showing the world how to transform vintage clothing into haute couture. Don't forget, I know a gal," she said, winking.

Callie's cheeks burned. From Adam's past comments, this was high praise from her future mother-in-law. "I don't know about that. I can't sew a straight seam, so I'm glad you think it looks okay."

Minna waved a hand, sending rainbows from her wide, diamond-incrusted wedding ring sparkling around the sunlit room. "Don't tell anyone, but I can't sew straight either. It doesn't ma—"

"Knock, knock." Adam's rich, deep voice carried from the open doorway. "May I come in?"

"Don't be silly, darling." Minna draped herself in the doorframe, blocking her son's entrance. "Everyone knows it's bad luck for the groom to see the bride before the ceremony."

Adam murmured something Callie didn't catch, and his mother sidestepped out of the way.

"Oh, all right. I suppose you did drive over here together this morning," Minna said, making a face.

He entered the room, and Callie did a double-take. Decked out in a tailor-made, charcoal gray suit, he threatened her peace of mind.

"Ah! You clean up rather well." Minna's pride was evident as she smoothed the collar of his white shirt.

Rather well? Try Understated Hotness R Us. Callie fought a ridiculous urge to throw his jacket wide and press herself against his broad chest. But something was missing. Her stomach sank a notch as she noticed his tie. Respectable but plain blue. No cartoon.

Was that an omen? An indication that he thought this marriage would be tedious and boring? If so, he was in for a rude awakening. Her life had been a lot of things, but boring wasn't one of them.

For the fifteenth time in the last half hour, she questioned whether she was doing the right thing.

"Hey, Ellie!" Gretchen smiled from ear to ear, shoving her flowers in a petite blonde's face as soon as the woman crossed to her side. "Look what I got!"

"They're awesome, Gretch." Eloise said, smiling.

Ugh. Backing out now would kill her little sister.

Callie might be doing the wrong thing, but she was doing it for the right reasons. That had to count for something.

Adam's gaze met hers, then traveled downward, making her toes curl inside her designer shoes. Sweet heaven. There ought to be a law.

When he raised his gaze again, it was admiring. "You look great, Cal." He took a few steps toward her, holding out a small blue box.

Her foolish heart did a double back flip and stuck the landing. "What's this?"

"My ring," he stated, matter-of-factly.

"Oh, right." They'd agreed to exchange rings since they played well into Adam's PR aims. Today, at breakfast, they had attempted to figure out a way they could slip on their own bands but had ended in defeat. It couldn't be done without a heaping helping of awkwardness.

After another full sniff of her flowers, Gretchen set her bouquet on a side table and joined them. "Do I get a present too?"

He gave her a wink and a wide smile. "I promised, didn't I?"

A swell of wonderment swept through Callie. Five years of working with him and she could count his genuine smiles on one hand. Yet he'd known Gretchen for less than twenty-four hours and was already teasing her while smiling like the Cheshire Cat. Such was the magic of her sister.

With a flourish, he reached into his pocket and withdrew a small drawstring bag.

Gretchen rose on tiptoe. "For me?" In seconds, she'd untied the straps and revealed a glass unicorn, no bigger than a quarter.

Callie blinked back tears. Such was the magic of the man she was marrying.

Gretchen cradled the unicorn in her palm. "She's so tiny!" Humming under her breath, she twirled around the room with the gift tucked into her palm, sending the blue silk of her full skirt flying.

Eloise caught her mid-twirl. "Let's take her downstairs while your sister finishes getting ready." She gave Callie a grin as she led Gretchen out of the room.

Callie smiled. "Thanks, Adam. You shouldn't have, but it's perfect. She loves it."

He shifted his weight and eyed the flowers she still held. "I see you've robbed the greenhouses, Mum."

"Of course." Minna stepped beside him and brushed at his lapel, sending more diamond sunbursts throughout the room. The woman was in constant motion, with a grace of movement Callie envied.

Minna frowned at her son and stuck her hands onto her hips. "I know you two want to downplay this marriage, but it's important to start things out properly."

Adam stretched an arm around his mother and gave her a squeeze, which she returned. The gesture was relaxed and comfortable, a moment both shared without conscious thought.

Once again, Callie wondered if he would become that comfortable with her at some point during their little bargain. Seeing him with his family revealed a new, softer side of him. A side that made her knees go weak and her heart go rogue.

He raised an arm and glanced at the fancy wristwatch he wore that did everything but cook his dinner. "I'll leave you to it, now. Don't get so caught up in things that you forget to come downstairs." He looked at his mother pointedly. "You know how punctual Granddad is."

Minna rolled her eyes and leaned close to Callie. "That man thinks five minutes early is ten minutes late."

Callie grinned as mother and son shared full-on laughs at the old man's expense before heading toward the door. Their easy affection was a far cry from the endless bickering that had characterized any gathering of her own family.

Freaking amazing.

Her gaze strayed to the big red numbers on the bedside alarm clock.

There was still time to run…

****

"Well, son, you have about five more minutes to change your mind." Patrick Hughes set a large hand on Adam's shoulder, his lined face conveying his seriousness and concern. "Your mother's convinced this marriage will work out well for you both, but she's the romantic of the family. My offer of a no-interest loan to Callie still stands. You don't have to go through with this if you don't want to."

Adam looked at his father, relieved he had come clean with both his parents as to this marriage arrangement. Honesty was always the best policy. Speaking of, the claim that his mother was the romantic in the family was laughable.

True, as a jurist, his dad had a reputation for being a tough nut to crack. More than one attorney had quaked in his boots while his father peppered the poor schmuck with cogent questions and a withering stare. In his private life, however, Patrick was as soft as a five-minute-old ice cream cone.

His father wasn't a fighter; he was a thinker. Things were constantly turning over in his mind, which made him a good foil for Adam's mother, who often blurted out just what she thought at the very moment she thought it. He was also generous. Adam knew that the offer to give Callie a loan was born from his dad's desire to present a son he adored with options, rather than a condemnation of the marriage that was about to take place.

"Thanks, Dad. I'd be lying if I told you I haven't gone back and forth on this, but the more I think about it, the more convinced I am that we're doing the right thing. While we both appreciate your offer, a loan causes more stress than it relieves because Callie fears it would take her a lifetime to pay it back. She and I work well together—have since Day One—and I don't see that changing once we're married. I respect her and value her opinions, which is more than a lot of marriages have going for them. I think, in the long run, this is best for us both."

There. The more he repeated it, the better it sounded. This could work. *Would* work.

Patrick gave Adam's shoulder a final squeeze. "That's good enough for me," he said, nodding. "You're right. More than a few couples have started out with less."

Adam couldn't help noticing his father's gaze stray to where Mason and his wife, Priscilla, stood making calf eyes at each other. Although they did their best to hide it, Adam knew the couple's whirlwind marriage troubled both his parents. Not because they didn't like Priss, but because they had doubts about how well the couple, who'd eloped three days after their initial meeting, knew each other.

"Callie and I have known each other for five years," he reminded his dad. "Any cracks in our relationship would be visible by now."

Patrick nodded again and gave him a tight smile. "I'm sure you're right. Time to go slip into my robe and gather my things." He pointed toward the living room. "Meet you in the flower shop in a few."

Chuckling, Adam turned toward the room's long bay window. It offered a gorgeous view of the sprawling back lawn and the shiny Potomac below. Today, the alcove sported an enormous canopy of live flowers, including white roses and a few others he couldn't name, that his mother had erected over the past few days.

While he admired his mother's engineering, the bower struck him as a bit ridiculous and way too bridal. He'd been on the verge of insisting it be dismantled when Callie'd spotted it. He'd never seen her speechless until that moment.

Despite his conviction that the canopy was frivolous, the awe it inspired in her touched him, even though she'd tried to downplay it afterward as her concussion talking. If her apartment and now his former guest room were any indication, Callie shared his mother's love for all things green and growing.

Besides, Gretchen loved it too. She had spent hours beneath it last night, alongside her caregiver, Eloise. To Adam's surprise, Jeep had joined in too, playing with Gretchen's family of unicorns as if he'd been doing it all his life. Only a true bastard would take the floral display away from Callie's delightful, imaginative sister, and Adam hadn't fallen quite that far.

Speaking of Callie, she had, to use his mother's

phrase, "cleaned up well" today, in a dress that hinted at ripe curves her office attire masked. Wearing the outfit, with the small chain of baby's breath woven into her upswept curls, she reminded him of a statuesque, mythical goddess.

Mythical goddess? He almost laughed out loud. One look at Callie in a clingy dress and he was waxing poetic with his tongue hanging out. Maybe he was the one with the concussion.

"C'mon, bro." Jeep's firm hand shackled Adam's forearm. "It's time, if you're still determined to do this."

"Right." Adam shook himself out of his reverie, his steps growing heavy as he neared the sweet-smelling arch. He was getting married.

Something he'd sworn over his wife's grave he would never do again.

But, as he had reasoned throughout the sleepless night before, it wasn't like this marriage was real. Legal, yes. Real, no. This was little more than a title bump, a jump from boss to husband and assistant to wife.

Wife. None of the images that word conjured had anything to do with Callie. In his heart, he was married to Mallory. Always would be.

He frowned at his shoes and fingered the smooth gold of the plain wedding ring in his pocket. He could still take his dad up on his offer, but could he do that to Callie? She was the most self-reliant person he'd ever met. It had cost her a lot to ask for help. Without the concussion, she might have remained silent. Taken another job and disappeared from his world.

His frown deepened. The office without her was a nonstarter. For the past five years his professional life had run without a hitch and, selfishly, he wouldn't give that up. He wouldn't cut and run.

Behind him, the low hum of voices faded, and someone giggled. He turned as Gretchen started down the makeshift aisle his mother had arranged between a handful of folding chairs. The sight of the girl's beaming smile made this marriage a no-brainer.

Callie came next, but where Gretchen's face showed nothing but delight, hers was marred by concentration, her gaze glued to her feet.

Shit. Callie was trying, before this small gathering of his family, to put her best foot forward. Literally.

The effort both touched and embarrassed him. Long ago, he'd stopped seeing her limp and scar, but to her they must be a big deal. He would have to remember that. For now, he tried to convey support in the weak smile he gave her as she reached his side. His attempt failed. She looked like she was a few seconds away from bolting.

But she hung in there, passing Minna her bouquet and placing her hands in his as his dad began the ceremony. Thank God, his father wasn't one of those officiants who droned on and on. In mere minutes, Adam had placed the gold ring on Callie's finger and received his own.

He stared down at the simple circle representing eternity. In their case, that meant two years or, at best, a few more. Not a lifetime. That fact clanged cold and callous in his head as his father ended what should have been sacred vows.

"I now pronounce you husband and wife. You may kiss the bride."

Adam raised an eyebrow at his father. *Seriously?* Had his dad granted that permission out of habit? He returned his gaze to Callie's but was unable to read her expression. "I forgot about this part," he whispered.

"It's okay. We can just…" her voice trailed away.

"Right." He should shake her hand, or maybe give her a peck on her cheek and be done with it.

Yet the overwhelming urge to kiss her blindsided him. And not a chaste little peck, either. A passionate kiss, long and hard, right on her tempting, coral-colored lips.

He dipped his head a fraction of an inch, ready to make that huge mistake, when his new bride stood on tiptoe and used those sexy lips to plant a chaste kiss just to the west of his mouth.

That was it. Game over. Thanks for playing. In the next moment, she turned away as if nothing out of the ordinary had happened. In seconds, she was swallowed up by the small group of well-wishers.

Adam stood up straight and took his father's outstretched hand. All for the best. No big deal. A more intimate kiss would have royally messed things up between them.

But he'd have bet his last dollar that she would have tasted damn good.

Chapter Five

The office looked as if a tornado had struck.

When Adam had said the office had been hard hit by whoever had attacked her, Callie couldn't picture exactly what he meant. Now, making her way through a sea of scattered papers and books to the archway between their conjoined offices, she surveyed the damage with a sinking heart. It would take her days to clean up the mess and even longer to organize it all.

"Whoever it was, they sure did a number on the place," Ron said, from the comparative safety of the hallway doorway. "I feel just awful about this, Cal. I've thought and thought, and I swear I didn't see anyone suspicious that morning. Any idea what they were searching for?"

She turned toward the security guard. The expression on his weather-beaten face reinforced the concern that had roughened his voice.

"Absolutely zip." She'd added an extra dose of sunshine to the words, hoping to allay the man's guilt.

It wasn't his fault some lunatic had declared war on their office and her head.

Hands on her hips, she glanced around again. "Don't worry, Ron. It gives me a good reason to go through some of this stuff and reorganize everything."

Ron grunted. "Don't know about that. You're the most organized person I know." He waved his hand at the disaster. "I know better than to offer to help. You'll do everything yourself like always. So, I'll leave you to it. Got police on every floor, but you holler if you need me."

She nodded as he disappeared into the hallway, his footsteps echoing down the empty corridor. There was still a good hour before the first classes began, but she had arrived early for two reasons. First, she was anxious to see the office. To categorize the damage, yes, but also to return to her work.

Her unexpected week off had been hijacked by doctor's appointments and wedding prep, and she wasn't accustomed to letting work slide for that long, especially given the chaos of the break-in. Monumental though the task might be, she was itching to get started on the clean-up.

She wasn't as proud of the second reason. Coward that she was, she had grabbed at the chance to avoid her new husband. Something she'd become pretty good at in the day and a half since her marriage.

The ceremony had gone off without a hitch. Well, almost. That awkward moment with the kiss had been weird, but they'd both slid past it unharmed. The lunch afterward had been incredible. Minna Hughes knew how to throw a party, even a small one.

But, despite their good intentions, the easy camaraderie of the Hughes family had taken its toll. Even Adam, by far the most austere member of the group, grew more approachable in his family's presence. Callie wasn't used to so much affection. Her entire life had revolved around two people, her sister and herself. She was comfortable with it being the two of them against the world. Add in anyone else, and it threw her for a loop.

So, when the wedding luncheon had finally wound

down, she'd changed her clothes and caught a ride back to Gretchen's, moving faster than a bat out of hell. Once there, she'd spent the rest of the day relaxing with her sister, safe and secure in her old life. A life where she didn't have to think about the ridiculously attractive man she'd married or the enchanting family that came with him.

Sunday had brought more of the same. If Adam thought it strange that his wife of twenty-four hours preferred his sister-in-law's company to his own, he hadn't mentioned it.

"I thought I'd find you here."

Speak of the devil. Callie jumped as Adam stepped into the office and began navigating his way across the messy floor. The sight of his lean, powerful hips, flexing against the slim fit of his tailored navy pants, rendered her momentarily speechless. Good Lord, he was fine.

"What are you doing here this early?" She managed to spit out the question only by fixating on the Snoopy and Woodstock tie he wore this morning. It hung neatly against his immaculate blue oxford shirt, the longer of its two triangle ends resting against the flat planes of his lower abdomen.

Her cheeks warmed as she raised her gaze back to his face. Marriage or no, she had to maintain her professionalism around him. Otherwise, he might put two and two together and she'd really be sunk.

"I figured you'd be anxious to get to work, so I headed in as soon as I'd finished at the gym."

Was that a faintly knowing look in his eyes? Searching his features through narrowed eyes, she had the distinct impression that he knew damn well she was trying to avoid him. Worse, that he found it amusing. She lifted her chin. It didn't matter. Nothing in their marriage arrangement dictated she spend her free time with him.

Turning, he set his computer case down on the corner of her desk and rubbed his hands together. His wedding band glinted in the fluorescent light. "Ready to get started?"

Callie bit her lip. Yes, she was more than ready to get started, but less than ready to plop down on the floor in front of him. Despite her own vigorous exercise routine, her hip didn't like to bend on command.

She avoided making such moves in front of others whenever possible. However, given the changes of the past week, it was silly to continue that practice around Adam. They'd be living together for at least the next two years.

With a heavy sigh, she leaned her back against the wall. Here went nothing. Stretching her bad leg straight out in front of her, she began to slide toward the floor as gracefully as possible.

A hand appeared in front of her face. Startled, she looked up. Adam's look was mild, devoid of any pity, but her long-standing habit of refusal was hard to break.

"Thanks, I'm good." By fits and starts, she slid the rest of the way down and arranged herself in a halfway comfortable position.

He withdrew his hand and inclined his head slightly. The movement caused an unruly dark curl to fall over one eye, making him look years younger. "Suit yourself. For the record, I don't bite."

Heat flooded her cheeks. "I know. I'm sorry, that was rude. I'm just not..." She bit into her lip again.

"Used to accepting help." In a fluid move, Adam crouched in front of her, his crooked grin taking the sting out of his words. "I know, remember?" His wide shoulders rose in a shrug. "Look, the wedding was awkward, to say the least. Between it and the attack on you, I've been on edge and, while you haven't complained, it must have been hard on you, too. How about we leave it all behind us and try to find our way back to normal again?"

Callie glanced at her own wedding band. The one he'd placed there. "It's a new normal."

Shrugging, he reached up and loosened his tie a fraction. "Yeah, well, it's not the first time I've had to start over."

The soft timbre of his voice belied the storm in his eyes. His cryptic comment begged questions that she didn't dare ask. Was he speaking of his wife's death, or some other event in his past? It didn't matter. He could keep his secrets. God knew, she'd move heaven and earth to keep hers.

"You're right." She nodded. "We can't go on this way."

He stuck his hand out again, this time to shake. "To a new normal?"

"To a new normal." She wrapped her fingers around his and ignored the tingle of intimacy. That was not part of their norm, old, new, or otherwise.

With an ease she envied, he rose to his feet again and surveyed the damage around them. "Believe it or not, this looked worse the other day." He gestured toward the empty bookcases that filled most of the wall space. "All of these were shoved away from the wall, as if the guy had looked behind them. What on earth would we hide *behind* a bookcase?" He pushed a hand through his hair. "I know I sound like a broken record, but none of it makes any sense. First of all, who picks one of the busiest times of day to rob a place? This place was crammed with students and staff. The guy took a big risk." Bending, he stacked up a few volumes and laid them on one of the shelves. "Second, what in the hell was he looking for?"

Callie looked up from the pile of papers she'd been shuffling through. There was zero chance Adam hadn't discussed the break-in with his family, but he'd kept it light with her until now, probably because she still couldn't remember jack-shit about what had happened one short week ago. Clearly, he was just as puzzled and concerned as she was.

"I have no idea. The only thing I can think of is that magazine article that came out last month. You remember," she continued at his questioning look, "the one mentioning the rumor about your family owning a Gutenberg Bible."

Adam made a face. "That story has been around for generations. It's a joke. If my family owned a Gutenberg, it would have surfaced long before now. I said as much in the article."

"*I* know that, and *you* know that, but a Gutenberg Bible is one of the most valuable volumes on the planet. What if someone really thinks you have one?"

He spread his arms, encompassing the small suite of offices. "And I keep a five-hundred-year-old book worth upwards of thirty-five-million dollars lying around in *here*?"

When he put it that way, it did sound far-fetched, but people got hung up on all sorts of wild ideas. "Well, you mentioned you've been researching lots of old manuscripts for the new textbook, and there's no way Joe

Magazine Reader would know those volumes are under lock and key in the campus library. Plus, no offense to Ron, but our security is a far cry from that at your grandfather's or your parents' place. Maybe our would-be thief thought this was a logical and easy place to start. You *are* the historian of the family."

Amusement flickered in Adam's eyes as he quirked an eyebrow. "You know that's crazy, right?"

Callie lifted a shoulder. "I'm not saying it makes sense, but it's the only thing I can think of."

Looking doubtful, he bent and scooped up another armful of books. "The police think the guy was a professional because he was able to toss the place so quickly and quietly." He shook his head. "Again, I'm a history professor, for God's sake. Why hire anybody, professional or not, to rob this place?"

"He must have been looking for something specific." She scanned the rooms, taking inventory. Adam had an impressive library and some of the books were quite old, but there was nothing worth stealing. "That's interesting... As far as I can tell, our desks are untouched. Most of the damage involves the bookcases."

"Hmm." He eyed the empty shelves. "I guess that's in line with your Gutenberg theory—what better place to hide a valuable book than a crowded bookcase?" Adam treated her to another boyish, lopsided grin that sent her heart knocking against her ribs. "Listen to me." He gave his tie another tug. "I'm talking like the Gutenberg idea is within the realm of possibility."

Callie sucked in a deep breath. God, he was cute. How freaked out would he be if she stood and walked right into his arms? A better question was how freaked out would she be? Beyond words. Instead, she stayed where she was, countering his grin with one of her own. "Maybe the shelves were pushed away from the walls in order to search for a safe or something."

His grin grew wider. "You're pretty good at this detective business. Maybe I should enlist your help with the next Wolfe Bridges plot."

He was joking, but she tingled anyway. Aside from proofreading his final edits, he never included her in his fiction writing process, which involved holing up in some quiet, picturesque little cottage somewhere each summer. The mere thought of being alone with him, away from the pressures of society and family, made her drool. He would be different, minus the intrusion of everyday life. His humor-filled writing told her that much.

She pushed aside the daydream. "I don't think I could be away from Gretchen for that long," Her sister was her number one priority. Always had been, always would be.

"There's no reason we couldn't look for a place big enough for her and Eloise, too." Adam's look grew guarded, and he cleared his throat. "But you're right, it would probably be best if you stayed here." He flicked back his cuff and glanced at his watch before he crossed to her desk and picked up his jacket and computer bag again. "I lost track of the time. I've got to run by the library to pick up some books before my freshman seminar this morning. Will you be okay by yourself while I'm in class?"

His words popped the fantasy taking shape in her head. Something to do with them entwined together upon the sand in some tropical paradise.

As if.

She fluttered a hand, shooing him toward the door. "Yes, of course. Go. Have fun terrifying all those freshmen. I'll be fine." One couldn't live in her old neighborhood and be faint of heart.

"Okay." For a moment he stood there, looking down at her, as if he had something else to say. Then, with a brief nod, he turned and left the room.

For a long moment, she remained still, willing her fantasy to return. Simply because Adam was off-limits in real life didn't mean a girl couldn't indulge in a few sexy beach dreams.

****

Adam took the long expanse of white marble steps three at a time. For a man with so many academic initials after his name, he'd just acted like a damn fool.

What on earth had possessed him to invite Callie along during his summer exile? Not to mention Gretchen and Eloise! That time was sacrosanct. He was unplugged, unreachable, and undisturbed. Just him and his imagination. Even his brothers were forbidden from tagging along.

He'd taken his first solo summer trip a few months after Mallory's death, hoping a new vista and some alone time would help ease his grief. Miraculously, they had. Away from well-meaning family and friends, he'd been able to mourn freely during that first trip.

Plus, the get-away had allowed him to write down— or more accurately, type into his computer—the spy story that had been knocking around in his head for years. He'd been pulling that summer escape hatch ever since, going wherever he wanted to go and doing whatever he wanted to do while he was away, including writing several best-sellers.

Once, he'd spent the whole day in his boxers. His mother would have had a heart attack if she'd known.

But that was just it. *No one* knew what he did when he was gone and, thank heaven, they were too polite to ask. In truth, he didn't do much, aside from writing. Some days he got so sucked in, he barely left his desk.

Nothing about his summer hiatus was sexy. He spent every hour he wasn't eating, sleeping, or exercising on work, and he loved every minute of it. Callie and his family could reach him if needed, but the unspoken rule was, unless someone's hair was on fire, he did the contacting.

The last thing he needed was Callie tagging along, distracting him.

He slowed his ascent up the stairs leading to the red-brick library's entrance. *Listen to yourself, man. When did Callie become a distraction?*

Since a bump on her head had turned his world upside down.

In a matter of days, he'd stopped viewing her as his pleasant, efficient personal assistant and started viewing her as a fun and attractive woman. Someone he enjoyed spending time with. Someone he'd like to know better. He was having a hell of a time remembering that wasn't part of their deal. Aside from the ring around his finger, nothing should have changed. But something had. Callie was now his *wife*, and that status conjured up all sorts of intimate and emotional reactions. It made what would be unethical in the professional realm possible in the private.

For his own peace of mind, he had to shut it down. Right here, right now. No more memories of how her vulnerability had tugged on his MIA heartstrings in the hospital. No more dwelling on how carefree she was, laughing with her sister. And most definitely, no more erotic guesses about the curves under that wedding dress she'd worn a few days before. Ever since, a swift kick of desire hit his stomach and began heading south every time he so much as glanced in her direction.

Damn fool.

Fortunately, he wasn't seventeen anymore. He could do this. He just had to concentrate on what really mattered. Like the break-in. As he'd told Callie, the idea that his family had managed to keep a Gutenberg Bible hidden for well over two centuries was just plain ridiculous.

But he couldn't ignore reality. The article had played up the old story and some people would believe anything. He had to admit it was possible—not probable, but possible—that some insane collector had the wrong idea.

At the top of the stairs, he detoured to one of the ancient iron benches sitting along the library's columned portico and pulled out his cell. As he so often reminded his students, when it came to history, primary sources were best.

"Hey, Grandad."

His grandfather's spry voice boomed through the earpiece like the veteran campaigner he was. "Adam! How's the new bridegroom? By golly, I like that young woman you married. Good head on her shoulders and pretty to match. Happy for you both."

"Thank you, sir," Adam said, ignoring the twinge of guilt his grandfather's heartfelt words provoked. At his parents' urging, he and Callie had agreed that there was no reason his grandfather needed to know the details surrounding their marriage. As far as the aging patriarch was concerned, theirs was a love match. "I wondered if you'd go over the Gutenberg story with me again. It's come up here at work, and I want to make sure I have the details right."

His grandfather laughed. "That old chestnut? I'm happy to retell it, but you know it's just family folklore."

"I do, but you tell the story better than Dad."

Another booming laugh came through the speaker. "Course I do! You can't beat an old windbag of a politician when it comes to telling stories."

This time, Adam joined in the laughter. He knew for a fact that his grandfather and his cronies spent hours swapping tales of past glories, some true and some not.

"Here's what my father told me. Originally, our family was German, although Germany didn't truly exist back then. I'm talking centuries ago—around 1717, or thereabouts. A group of German miners, including my several-times-great-grandfather, Fritz Hutman, got fed up with things in the motherland and headed to the then British colony of Virginia. They liked what they saw, settled in, and founded a town called Germanna. Inventive, weren't they?"

"They did add the 'n' and the 'a'," Adam pointed out with a laugh.

"That's true. Well, it didn't take long for Fritz to become disillusioned with mining. Within five years, he left the mines and settled here, in what became Germantown, Virginia." The old man chuckled. "Another inspired name. It was Fritz who built what's become the central part of the farmhouse."

Adam pictured his parents' cozy family room, with its massive stone fireplace and chinked logs running along one long wall. "Right."

"Old Fritzie, he could read and write, and he kept a journal. Of course, it's in German, but the family had an English copy made on what would've been his hundredth birthday. You've seen it, and it'll come to you when I'm gone, since you're the historian."

"Thanks," Adam said, honored. "I'll take good care of it."

"You're welcome, son. Now, where was I? Ah, yes. Periodically, Fritz referenced a family Bible, usually when he had births or deaths to record, et cetera. Aside from that, I won't lie to you, his journals are deadly dull. Filled with the weather and how his crops were doing."

Adam smiled. One man's junk was an historian's treasure.

"So, fast-forward a couple of generations and that puts us smack-dab in the middle of the Civil War. All of a sudden, in another journal, this one written by Fritz's great-great-grandson, the family Bible is being touted as a rare 'Gutenberg.' History lover that you are, I don't have to tell you what that means. Of course, the chances that it really was one of the few that Gutenberg ran on that press of his are slim to none. What's important is the family *believed* the volume had value—real, monetary value, I mean. In fact, they start referring to it as the 'family treasure.' All of this becomes a concern, of course, because the family were abolitionist Yankees and the Confederate Army was milling about, threatening to take the house and farm. They didn't want to leave anything else of value behind that the Rebs could get their hands on. Losing their home was bad enough."

Adam nodded. "I can only imagine."

John Hughes grunted. "Exactly. So, with Johnny

Reb breathing down their necks, the family flees to the North after hiding this so-called 'Gutenberg' somewhere on the property. They didn't want to risk traveling with it, seeing how old it was." The old man's sigh echoed down the phone line. "And that's pretty much it. Shortly after the war, the next generation reclaimed the house and land. Incidentally, that's when the Hughes line begins, thanks to a Northern marriage."

Adam ran a hand through his hair and whistled. "That's quite a story, Grandad. I never grow tired of hearing it. Did you ever look for the Bible personally?"

"Hell, no," his grandfather roared. "I grew up at the tail-end of the Great Depression, and I had better things to do with my time than go treasure-hunting. All I can say is, if a previous generation hid a Bible anywhere, Gutenberg or not, they did a first-rate job of it. My brother, Adam, for whom you're named, was obsessed by it. He'd rush through his chores, higgledy-piggledy, just so he could go dig holes here and pull up floorboards there. Just about drove our poor mother crazy."

A poignant note had crept into the old man's voice, no doubt caused by the memory of his boyhood days, before his only brother had been killed in World War II.

"So, you don't think there's any way the story could be true?"

His grandfather paused before answering. "I just don't see how," he said at last. "If you look at the journals, it's intriguing that they begin referring to the Bible by the 'Gutenberg' name, as if they know what they're talking about. But for something like that to remain hidden for over one hundred and fifty years... No. That's just too hard to swallow."

"I'm sure you're right. Thank you for sharing it all

with me, again, sir. I appreciate it."

"Of course. Always good to talk with you. Now, it's time for my morning nap. I know it's not even eight o'clock, but I've already been up for three hours. It's hell getting old. Can't sleep when you're supposed to, but you're dozing off the rest of the time. Give that new bride of yours a kiss for me."

"Will do." With that small lie, Adam dismissed the call.

No matter where he went these days, all his roads led back to Callie. Kissing Callie. He stood and slipped his phone into one of the many pockets of his computer case, his mind stuck on an image of her lush lips.

Damn fool.

Chapter Six

"You're amazing."

Callie laughed at Adam's dazed expression and glanced around the office. Slowly but surely, the two rooms were beginning to resemble their former selves. "I'm not done yet." She held up a stack of books. "I still have the Early Republic shelves to finish, and I haven't even started on the Civil War books."

"Yeah, but I can see the floor again." He walked over to her and ran a finger along the edge of a nearby shelf.

Mmm. As usual, he smelled good, his spicy cologne mingling with a hint of the crisp, autumn air he'd just walked through.

"Here." Facing her, he slid the books from her grasp and set them on the corner of his desk. "You've done more than enough for today. It's four o'clock, and I'm willing to bet you didn't stop for lunch."

She pretended offence, then broke into a grin. "You'd win that bet." Now that he mentioned it, her stomach was a little hollow.

His eyes glinted with humor. "Let me guess, you were—"

"On a roll," they finished together, laughing.

"You know how I get with a big project like this." She set her hands on the top of her head and stuck up her forefingers, as if they were bull's horns. "Head down and just go."

"You're a force of nature," he agreed. "How about dinner out as a 'thank you'? You've more than earned it. I can call Jake Calhoun and see what he can do."

Callie's jaw dropped, both at the name and the casual way Adam said it. "Jake Calhoun, as in world famous, former White House chef, Jake Calhoun?"

She recognized the name, of course, but had never eaten at the chef's eponymous five-star restaurant in Georgetown. Even if it had been within her budget, it was impossible to get a table.

Adam flashed an embarrassed grin. "That sounded less pretentious in my head, but I take it you're impressed?"

She laughed. Self-deprecating humor was one of his most endearing qualities. "Yes, I admit I am. The menu is supposed to be off the charts. Do you eat there often?"

The question was a stark reminder of how little he'd revealed about his private life and how different it was from hers. He'd made it clear from the start that personal matters were out-of-bounds.

Now, thanks to their new arrangement, his life outside the office was literally part of her job description, a pinch-worthy thought if there ever was one. Not that she was kidding herself. This invite was less about time with her and more about his plan to be spotted, as a *married* man, about town. Still, the vision of herself parading through Calhoun's on Adam Hughes's arm caused quivers in the darndest places.

What a difference a week made.

"I won't lie," Adam said, nodding. "You know I try to avoid public places, but if I'm going out, chances are I'm going to Jake's. The food is *that* good. Plus, he and my dad grew up together. He's a terrific guy, arranges take-out for me when I'm not in the mood to battle the photographers." His eyes darkened. "They all wait, waist deep, outside the place," he cautioned, giving her a questioning look. "Do you feel up to it?"

She gave him a grin. "For dinner at Calhoun's, I'd walk over hot coals."

"Great." He searched his cell. "The paparazzi are banned from entering the restaurant, so once we're inside, we'll have some peace. What time do you want to eat?"

She looked down at her black leggings and long, peasant-style blouse. They weren't even up to her usual business attire standards, let alone five-star restaurant appropriate. "I'd like to shower and change. Does six work?"

He nodded and spoke into his phone. "Jake? Oh, yeah. Thanks. Mmm-hmm." He gave her a playful frown and made a rolling gesture with his hand, as if to speed up the conversation. "No, we've known each other a long time, just kept it under wraps… Yeah. I thought we might grab dinner there tonight. Can you squeeze us in around six? Great." He gave her a thumbs up. "No, that's okay. We'll have to face them sooner or later… Okay. See you then."

He disconnected and flashed a grin at her. "No hot coals necessary tonight. You're sure you're ready to face the vultures?"

"Yep." She glanced down at her watch with a stab of panic. That gave her an hour and a half to make it to the apartment, shower, and find something in her limited wardrobe that would pass for dinner out with the hot male in front of her. It was time to get moving. Showing her aching hip who was boss, she sidestepped around

Adam and retrieved her purse from her bottom desk drawer.

He tilted his head toward his office. "I have a few things to finish up here. Do you need a ride? I can call you a car."

She waved a hand. "No need. I'm a Metro kind of girl. Always have been, always will be. Besides, it's faster at this hour."

He hesitated, then nodded, flooding her with relief. He could take her out of her crappy apartment, but that was all she'd allow. That and dinner at a gourmet restaurant.

"Meet you back home, then."

Home. Ha! It still felt more like a hotel, but she nodded anyway, slid her bag over her shoulder, and high-tailed it out the door. Classes were in session, so the hallway and stairs were empty, save the occasional student roaming here and there, and she made her way through the building in record time. Even the expansive lawn of the campus quadrangle, now turning a lackluster brown and blanketed by crunchy leaves, was devoid of people willing to brave the chill in the air.

In DC, the autumn weather often changed in a heartbeat, and she walked, at the best of times, about as fast as a slug. As a result, Callie always kept a lightweight jacket within her cavernous purse. With the persistent wind stinging her eyes, she dug it out and slipped it on, grateful for the added warmth it provided. Adjusting the jacket's hood over her flyaway hair, she spotted a lone figure out of the corner of her eye. He was a thin, nondescript man, dressed in jeans and a dark hoodie. The hood was up, and he wore a pair of sunglasses despite the decided lack of sunshine.

Sunglasses aside though, there wasn't anything that unusual about him. Yet warning bells began blaring in her head.

Okay, now you're just scaring yourself. If she was going to freak out every time she saw a dude in sunglasses and a dark sweatshirt, she would have to quit her job. Shrugging off her unease, she resumed her slow but steady trek to the nearby Metro stop, enjoying the exercise after the long day cooped up, cleaning. A quick, backward glance confirmed the man had followed her into the large parking lot, but now lagged, his attention on his cellphone.

Relief flooded through her. *Good.* He wasn't tailing her, and she could dismiss him from her mind. Nothing was going to kill her mood. After all, she was dining at Calhoun's tonight.

With the drop-dead gorgeous Adam. Freaking. Hughes.

What could possibly go wrong?

****

"What is it?" His employer's voice was laden with frustration. "I thought I told you *I* do the calling. The one thing you did right was plant that bug in Hughes' office. They just decided to go out tonight. You ready, or do I have to do your job for you?"

"Um, yeah. I'm ready." The man in the hoodie shivered as a blast of icy wind shot straight through his sweatshirt. "I just wanted to go over it one more time." He winced as he spoke, bracing for the blistering response that was sure to follow.

It did. After a good half a minute of swearing and insults, the hoarse voice on the other end of the line returned to a more reasonable tone. "You meet my man as soon as you see them leave. You're not to toss the place, you understand? Not like last time. No one's to know you were there."

"Right. No problem. How do I recognize your guy?"

A heavy sigh echoed down the line. "What do you want, a code word or something? I already told you; he'll be looking for you. You don't have to say a word—better if you don't. He'll give you access to the penthouse elevator and make sure you get in and out without being detected. Your job—your *only* job—is to get me what I want. And for God's sake, wear gloves."

The man fisted the strings on his hoodie and gritted his teeth. This wasn't his first rodeo, and he didn't need to be told how to do his fucking job. But he swallowed his anger and played nice.

"Okay. You got it," he said, with a liberal dose of enthusiasm. "I'll be in and out, like a ghost."

"See that you are."

He opened his mouth, ready with another, not quite so peppy response, but the connection had been severed. It was just as well. A shiver rippled through him again, and this time it had nothing to do with the weather. He was on slippery ground. The man who'd hired him hadn't been any too pleased to hear how the office break-in had gone. The apartment, though, would be deserted. Much more his style. He'd be less rushed, more thorough.

Fact was, he'd never been involved in such a high-class operation before. This guy had eyes and ears everywhere. Inside informants, phone taps, office bugs. He knew everything about everybody.

It was a far from comforting thought.

****

Adam caught himself glancing across the hired car's expansive backseat in Callie's direction. Again. Even in the strobe-like flashes of the passing streetlights, the play of emotions across her face was fascinating. She was happy. Vibrant. Entertaining.

Sexy.

Apparently, he'd been living under a rock for the past five years. He'd been aware of Callie, of course. Just not...*sexually* aware. His eyes had left his head when she stepped into the living room tonight. The green of her dress matched her eyes perfectly. Its neckline was just low enough to give an eyeful of pale shoulders and a hint of full breasts. After a week, the shiner had faded to a slight purple smudge, and she made no attempt to camouflage it or the long scar that ran along one jawline. As a result, the thin white line became little more than a slight indentation, far less noticeable than it would be if covered by a trowel-full of makeup.

Shit. There he went again, noticing details he shouldn't be noticing. They shared a name, a house, and some private time. It didn't mean she was interested in him. It shouldn't mean he was interested in her. Whatever the mental equivalent of a cold shower was, he needed one, pronto, so he began searching through photos on his phone. A much-admired plate of lasagna. His mum and dad at Mason's last birthday. *Perfect.* His digital scrapbook was doing its job, tamping down on any errant urges.

Laughing at himself, he zeroed in on a photo of Jeep's slobbery dog, Darrow. *Even better.* Darrow was a lot of things, but a turn-on was not one of them.

"How far to the restaurant?" Callie asked, bracing herself as they neared a stop sign.

It was clear their driver was a student of the accelerate-like-hell-then-brake school of driving.

Adam grinned and reached for his own grab handle. "We're almost there."

As if on cue, the vehicle leaped ahead, then drew to a whiplash stop alongside the curb as the driver announced their destination. In seconds, a cluster of sleazy gossipmongers aimed their cameras at the black sedan. *Bastards.*

Adam paid the driver via the app before facing Callie. She appeared unfazed by the activity surrounding the car. He, on the other hand, wished they'd opted for take-out instead. "Ready?"

Her eyebrows lifted in surprise. "Sure. You told me I could just be myself, and I've had lots of practice with that."

He managed a rumble of laughter and reached for the door handle. "If only it were that simple."

His muscles tensed, as if he were walking into a prizefight instead of exiting a car. Ignoring the flurry of clicks, flashes, and whirs, he circled to Callie's side. The barrage of questions hurled in their direction struck him like so many bullets.

"It's Adam Hughes. Hey, Adam! Is this her?"

"Is this the new wife?"

"Turn this way, Adam!"

"Mrs. Hughes! Over here."

With the grace of one to the manor born, Callie gave the press a casual wave. Then, she linked her arm with his and tugged him toward the restaurant.

"Nothing to see here, folks. Just an old married couple going out for dinner." She smiled as they passed through the ranks.

"How did he propose, Callie?"

"Have you known each other long?"

"How does it feel to be married to the Sexiest Man in America?"

Adam rolled his eyes at the last question. He'd never live down the ridiculous moniker some magazine had pinned on him years ago.

Callie gave his arm a squeeze and shot him a sultry look that could have singed the hair off his head. He'd suggested just that kind of look while they had waited for the car to pick them up, but he hadn't figured on the gut-punch it packed.

"I keep pinching myself," Callie said to one paparazzo. "His proposal left me speechless," she continued, pointing at another. "Yes, as I think you know, we've worked together for several years. Now, I appreciate you're just doing your jobs, but I'm starving. Rumor has it the food here's pretty good." She gave yet another reporter an exaggerated wink.

Then, she turned up the wattage of her smile and the most incredible thing happened: the paparazzi parted like the Red Sea.

Damn. With a few playful words and a well-timed wink, she'd managed what years of scowling, cursing, and once, right after Mallory's death, even a badly thrown punch had failed to do.

She'd tamed the press.

He should have known. Through the years she'd handled everyone, from terrified freshmen to his grumpy publicist, with total competence. He'd taken her calm, her capability, for granted. So, what had changed? Why was he so bowled over by her tonight?

Because tonight they were a couple.

The realization sent him tripping over his own feet. Without missing a beat, Callie steadied him with another brief squeeze of his arm.

She *steadied* him. Supported him. Guided him. Made him better. Had done for years but he'd been too self-absorbed to notice.

Shit. If he wasn't careful, he might just fall for this woman. Hard.

Good God. Overreacting much? He forced himself to relax. It must be the writer in him conjuring up such drama. After all, he was finished with relationships. Didn't want one and didn't need one. Mallory had been it—the big love of his life. But it was another good reminder not to let his inner storyteller create something out of nothing. They had a business deal, and that was it.

Callie released his arm once the restaurant's double doors swung closed. The maître' d, a transplanted Irishman named Ronan, greeted them with a wide smile, cradling a couple of menus in the crook of his arm. In a matter of seconds, they were seated at Adam's preferred table, tucked into the shadows of the restaurant's back corner.

She sank into one of the oversized wingchairs that were a Calhoun trademark and made a fanning motion with a hand. "Wow. Now I know why you call them 'vultures.' That was crazy. I was so nervous; I said the first thing that popped into my head. Was it okay?"

Adam sat and stared at her for a long moment. Her eyes glistened with uncertainty and her mouth bore no curve whatsoever. She had no idea how terrific she'd been. A twinge of guilt assailed his midsection. Was that so surprising? Hadn't he wondered how well she'd handle the bastards too?

Oh, ye of little faith.

"Yeah, it was great." Scant praise, but he didn't want to gush. Lowering his eyes, he pretended to study the menu. He had it memorized, but the heavy, leather-bound card put a nice barrier between them in the intimate setting.

After a minute, he looked across the table and caught her chewing her upper lip. To hell with it. She deserved an "atta girl" for her flawless performance. "No, really. You were perfect. Handled them exactly the right way."

She sighed and lifted her full water goblet. "Thank goodness. I figured the best way to tame them was to act pleasant while downplaying things as much as possible." After a long sip of water, she continued. "You hate them, don't you?"

He frowned. "Hate is a strong word, but I have a long history with them. Most of it's bad. After my wife died, they were disgusting. Followed me everywhere, even hung out at her grave." The memory made him shudder.

She nodded. "Fair enough. That was a huge intrusion at a time when you were suffering."

The understatement made him laugh. *More like ripped apart.* "Yeah. Now, whenever I'm around them, a part of me goes back to the rawness I felt then. I guess I don't hide my animosity very well."

With her left hand, she gave him a so-so wobble. Her wedding band glinted in the soft light. "Your whole demeanor changes. You become, I don't know. Rigid, I guess, and you have this killer look."

He frowned. "Un-uh. Mum and Jeep have The Look. It skipped me."

Her laugh floated across the table. "You couldn't be more wrong. You totally have The Look."

"Huh." Grinning, he shrugged. This was fun, almost flirty. Having a nice, relaxed dinner together was major progress after the tension-filled past few days. "Good to know. I'll try not to use it too much."

She dropped her gaze, running a finger around the base of her water goblet while gnawing at that same corner of her upper lip, now devoid of the glossy pink lipstick she wore. "It isn't any of my business, but I've noticed that the rest of your family tend to be more tolerant of the press. They don't get angry, and they're treated reasonably well in return. That's why I decided to act like it was no big thing."

His hackles rose and it took concentration to subdue what he now knew was The Look. "So, what? You think I should laugh and joke with them like Mason does? Give them idiotic nicknames, like 'Jimmy Olson' and 'Murrow,' the way Jeep does?"

"No, of course not. That's not you. I just suspect that the more you fight them, the more relentless they become."

Adam fiddled with the salt and pepper shakers for a moment, pushing them closer to the edge of the table. "I appreciate the thought."

He did. Right from the start, regardless of his persona and her inexperience, Callie had never been anything but straight with him, and he returned the honesty.

"But, with all due respect, you haven't lived with them for as long as I have." The Look surfaced again, and he forced himself to loosen up, giving her another grin. "However, I'll try and relax a little."

A pleased smile lit her face. "That's all a girl can ask."

"Adam! My man." Jake Calhoun sauntered up to the table in his chef's whites.

As usual, his toque threatened to slide off his head of bushy gray hair and his wire-rimmed cheaters were askew. The man looked like a train wreck, but he cooked like a dream. Adam stood, exchanging first a fist bump, then a bear hug with this long-time family friend.

"You must be Callie." Jake kissed his fingers in a chef's kiss, a gesture Adam recognized as the older man's full endorsement. "No wonder Adam's been hiding you. You're every bit as lovely as your name."

Her long eyelashes flickered. Adam understood. Compliments, even benign ones, made her uneasy.

He cleared his throat. "Speaking of happily married, is Oliver here tonight?" he asked, scanning the restaurant for Jake's husband.

"No. He has a performance tonight." Jake turned back to Callie. "My husband is first chair violinist for the National Orchestra," he said, pride puffing his already full cheeks. He flicked back his sleeve and checked his watch. "I don't mean to be rude, but I'm out of here shortly, so I can catch the show. Just wanted to say 'hello,'" he said, motioning to a waiter.

"Take care of these folks, Colin. They're family." After another admiring glance in Callie's direction and a thumbs-up for Adam, Jake sped off toward the kitchen.

They listened to Colin's spiel, and Callie ordered the house's signature pork tenderloin with spicy blueberry salsa. As mouthwatering as tonight's specials sounded, Adam couldn't quite bring himself to abandon his mainstay, an Italian roulade so melt-in-your-mouth delicious it would make angels weep.

Unusually tongue-tied, he cast about for something to talk about. He'd just about resorted to that old standby, the weather, when a charcuterie plate arrived at the table, with Jake's compliments. Callie's eyes grew wider than usual as she took in the overflowing slate slab.

"Oh, my God, it's gorgeous!" She covered her mouth with a hand as soon as the words were out.

He read her blush even in the dim light. Ducking, she leaned forward a little. The lavender scent she wore mingled with the tantalizing smells of the food. In fact, he didn't know which one made him hungrier.

"I'll let you in on a little secret," she said. "This is the fanciest restaurant I've ever been to, hands down."

Adam looked down at the plate in front of them. Her confession humbled him. He'd grown up eating well, in luxurious surroundings with the proverbial silver spoon. But that kind of living came with a hefty price tag, and if her apartment was anything to go by, Callie had never known that kind of extra. A sudden urge welled in him, to show her the very best this town had to offer. Whether it was an evening at the theater or a night in a five-star hotel, he'd enjoy the pleasure of viewing it through her eyes.

Careful. That sounded way too much like dating.

"I have a lot to be thankful for. No, no." He reached for her hand as she started to withdraw and held it beneath his own. Her skin was soft and warm, a stark reminder of how devoid of feminine touches his life had become. He loved his mother, but she simply didn't count.

"It's okay," he continued. "I'd be lying if I didn't admit my life's been…"

"Cushy?" The thin line of freckles across her nose danced.

Cute. Had they ever smiled this much with one another? Another warning sound went off in his head.

"Cushy," he agreed, provoking more freckle-dancing. "That sounds about right."

Her gaze slid down to their hands. Clearing his throat, he removed his, settling back into the chair. Distance. It had served him well since Mallory's death.

Callie helped herself to a piece of cheese, rolling her eyes in obvious ecstasy as she chewed. The look was so dramatic, he couldn't hold back another laugh. Blushing, she joined in, the low, throaty sound lowering his tension and ratcheting up his blood pressure, all at the same time.

She dabbed at her mouth with her napkin, then opened her eyes wide. "Oh, I meant to tell you. I thought I spotted the guy who attacked me, out in the quad today."

"What?" Adam gripped the chair arms. "Talk about burying the lead, Cal! Why didn't you tell me earlier?"

She raised both hands. "Hold your fire. I'm probably just being paranoid. I saw a guy in a hoodie and sunglasses and my imagination kicked into overdrive. For a hot minute, I thought he was following me, but he wasn't."

Adam raised his eyes to the ceiling, torn between strangling her or wrapping her in a bear hug. "That's it. You don't go anywhere alone until we catch the guy."

In the soft light, he sensed rather than saw her stiffen. After all these years, he should know better than to try and order her around, even if it was for her own protection. "Sorry, that was high-handed of me."

"You think?"

Grateful for the flash of humor in her eyes, he sighed. "Yeah. But I also think you need to be careful." He searched for softer words, deciding to go with a request instead of a tell. "How about this? I would appreciate it if you'd let me tag along with you for a bit. We still don't have any idea what this guy's agenda is. He hurt you once; he might do it again."

She touched the side of her head. Mason had removed her stitches the day before, and she claimed she felt just fine, but the cut, hidden under that mass of hair, was certainly still healing.

"Since you put it so nicely, I agree with you. Ever since I saw him today, I've been having these little flashbacks. I can remember someone similar following me into the office that day. I'm pretty sure I asked if he had an appointment."

"Okay. That's good, I guess. Better to remember. Look, I hate to spoil the evening, but I think we should tell the police about this, as well as campus security. I'd rather call them from the privacy of the apartment. I'll have them wrap up our dinner to go." He reached into his inside jacket pocket for his phone.

Callie nodded at the charcuterie tray and popped another piece of cheese into her mouth. "Once again, you're right. I'm sure—"

His phone vibrated, and he glanced down at the screen, doing a double take when he read the caller ID. Frowning, he met Callie's eyes.

"What? Who is it?" she asked.

"Believe it or not, it's the police."

Chapter Seven

"I'm sorry, Mrs. Hughes—I don't know what happened. All of a sudden, sirens were wailing, lights were flashing, and I couldn't shut the damn thing off."

"It's okay, Bill. There doesn't appear to be anything missing." Callie gave Bill Dobbs, the building's rotund head of security, an automatic smile as she looked around the living room.

In all honesty, she wasn't familiar enough with Adam's apartment yet to make that kind of determination. However, she wasn't about to say so. No way did she want this shifty-eyed man knowing she was still a stranger in her own home.

For nearly an hour, police officers and Secret Service agents had swarmed the apartment, doing all kinds of techy-CSI investigation. She didn't have the words to describe it. Surreal. Freaky. Insane. Things were going from bad to worse, and she couldn't help but wonder if the universe might be against this marriage agreement of theirs.

"Everything looks okay in the bedrooms," Adam confirmed, crossing through the kitchen and halting at her side. He met her gaze, his own full of concern, and set a hand on her shoulder. "Doing okay?"

His voice was low, his hand comforting. She fought the urge to curl up against the solid length of him and nodded. "I'm fine. A little shaken, that's all."

As if reading her mind, he rubbed her back before

tucking her close to his side.

A lifetime of self-reliance be damned. Just this once, she leaned into him, relishing the warmth and support of his hard body. This was an extenuating circumstance, that was all. It didn't mean she'd make a habit of it.

"That makes two of us." Adam's low voice held a note of puzzlement she sympathized with completely.

Moving in half inches, she wrapped her arm around his trim waist. There. Just as she'd told the press. A regular old couple, united in the face of a threat. No ulterior motive on her part at all.

"Did you see anything, Bill?" Adam asked.

The security man shook his head. "Nah, nothin', Dr. Hughes. It's like I was telling your wife here, the alarm started blaring, and I couldn't shut it off. Master code didn't work. Guess you have a second alarm, huh?" His dark, squinty eyes surveyed the room as he emitted a yappy little laugh that reminded Callie of a Yorkie her grandmother had owned.

"You hidin' a Picasso up here or something?" Again, the annoying laugh rang out.

Beside her, Adam tensed. He'd already warned her that he wasn't a fan of Dobbs, who appeared heavy on machismo and light on attention to his job. In fact, Adam had shared that he'd gone so far as to speak to the building management about their new hire, but they'd assured him the man was tops in his field and highly recommended. If today was anything to go by, however, Callie leaned toward Adam's point of view.

"You're new here." Adam's voice was razor sharp. "My grandfather stays here overnight when he has business in the city, so the Secret Service installed another alarm. The private elevator still works with an authorized building card key, but the second alarm must be deactivated in the elevator by a hidden handprint scanner. In other words, no one can sneak up to my— our—apartment. Knowledge of the alarm is on a need-to-know basis. Period. And you didn't need to know."

Ouch. Callie didn't move, for fear Adam would withdraw, but she sensed Bill was getting a taste of The Look.

The security man shuffled his feet. "Guess that explains the Suits," he said, and scratched his scruffy chin.

"Well." She gave Bill another smile. She didn't like the man, but she pitied anyone on the receiving end of Adam's glare. "Between the police and all these agents, I'm sure they'll figure it out. Security systems can be glitchy."

Ha. She didn't believe that for a minute, not with this state-of-the-art system. Someone had tried to enter this apartment. But why?

At that moment, an expressionless woman of about forty, wearing a dark gray business suit that screamed "Fed," crossed through the kitchen and entered the living room. Callie experienced a twinge of envy, watching the woman move with unmistakable authority. Oh, to be so sure of oneself.

"Dr. and Mrs. Hughes?" The agent handed out business cards with a curt nod. "Special Agent Andrews. We've confirmed someone entered your home. The elevator was activated, by key card, at 6:08 p.m. and the Secret Service alarm was triggered fifteen seconds later, when no handprint registered. That sent off the sirens here as well as alerting the responding federal offices. It's near deafening, and the perp left almost immediately by way of the elevator again."

The woman's recitation of this information was clipped and emotionless, which Callie found oddly reassuring. The facts themselves, however, were another story, and they had her stomach doing backflips.

Dobbs looked shaken as well. "Now, that's real strange." He ran a hand over his beard again.

Agent Andrews' sharp gaze transferred to the security man. "We'll need a list of everyone with card key access."

He raised his beefy hands. "Of course, of course. No problem." He jutted his chin toward the elevator. "You guys have a camera in there too, huh? I'll admit it. Ours has been on the blink for a day or two."

A muscle in the agent's jaw jumped. "That's unfortunate. We'll need access to the system anyway, to see if anything is recoverable."

Dobbs took a step backward. "Sure, you'll get it. Don't get your panties in a bind."

The agent's eyes narrowed into a killer look of her own.

A thousand watts of electricity shot through Callie as Adam ran his hand down over her shoulder and along her upper arm. *Holy crap.* She had to stop reacting this way. She snatched a peek up at him, but his attention remained trained on the agent.

Okay. Good to know. This attraction was a one-way street. Adam hadn't so much as blinked at a caress that had rocketed her through the roof.

"This sounds like an inside job." Adam's voice couldn't have sounded any colder. "Any ideas, Bill?"

The man sucked air in between his teeth. "Let's see... We've had some construction going on down on two. It's possible one of the guys got his hands on a key card. Or gals," he added, with a patronizing glance at Andrews. "Don't mean to leave out the ladies."

Callie's fingers itched with a desire to slap his sexist face. As if reading her mind, Adam's arm tightened, keeping her tethered to his side.

"Like I said, we'll be looking at *everyone* who has building access." The agent's emphasis was unmistakable.

Dobbs' smile slipped. He scratched his neck one more time, then sidestepped toward the elevator. "Right. Well, if there isn't anything else, I'll get back to my office and start on that list."

Both Adam and Andrews nodded, and the security man joined several agents and a policewoman in the elevator. The faint smell of sweat hovered in Dobbs' wake. Callie saw Andrews send a meaningful glance at another agent, who ducked into the private, emergency stairwell. It looked as if Dobbs had piqued the Secret Service's interest. That was no surprise. There was something hinky about the man.

"The police and Secret Service are assisting, sir," Andrews told Adam. "But the Agency's taking the lead. We've briefed the president's security team, and they're taking additional precautions on their end." She paused to scan the room. "As far as your apartment goes, I'd take comfort from that alarm system. It did its job well."

Adam pushed his free hand through his hair, leaving it standing on end. "Great. We appreciate it."

The elevator doors reopened, and Andrews and the remaining policeman stepped in. "Let me know if you have any questions or concerns," the agent said.

"Absolutely. Thanks."

"Thank you. Goodnight," Callie said. Before the elevator doors were closed, a heavy dose of reaction set in, and she ground her jaw shut as her teeth began to chatter. First the office, now the apartment. What the hell was going on?

She ducked away from Adam's sheltering arm. One thing was clear. They were alone now, so he had no need to play the role of Anxious Husband.

Besides, standing that close to him, experiencing each flex and ripple of his muscular arm and torso, made her a little too willing to play the role of Very Lustful Wife.

She headed toward the couch, making no attempt to hide her limp. "Holy crap, Adam. I don't mind sharing that I'm freaking out. Do you think someone's really after your grandfather?" A blast of fidgets hit her stomach as she collapsed onto the white cushions.

He faced her squarely, hands on his narrow hips. "I have no idea. But if, God forbid, Gramps is the target, what was the attack on you and the tossing of the office all about? My grandfather's never even been there."

Callie didn't scare easily, but this hit way too close to home. "I suppose it's too much of a coincidence to believe the two break-ins are unrelated?"

He raised an eyebrow. "What do you think?"

She sighed. Her hip ached from being on her feet so long, and her head was beginning to do the same. "I think they're related."

The admission left her forlorn. In an effort to assuage the feeling, she hugged one of the black throw pillows to her midsection. Of course, it would have been nicer to be hugging Adam, but she wouldn't—she really wouldn't—wish for what she couldn't have.

He took a hard look around. "I can't understand what it is he or she is looking for. I mean, the Gutenberg idea is just plain ridiculous." Slipping his hands into his pants pockets, he paced, his large strides propelling him across the room in seconds. "There's no 'why' to all this."

She leaned back into the couch's softness and closed her eyes. "You're right." But she was too tired to puzzle it out. Right now, anything, including climbing Mt. Everest, sounded easier than solving this mystery.

The rattle of a plastic bag caused her to open her eyes again. Adam was spreading an assortment of plastic containers out on the breakfast bar.

"I promised you dinner," he said, waving her over. "It's lukewarm but will still taste good. I don't know about you, but I'm starving."

She struggled to her feet. In truth, she didn't have much of an appetite, but she was all for the distraction. "Okay."

Joining him at the counter, she picked up her forgotten dinner and a set of the plastic utensils the restaurant had included with the food.

They settled into their usual places at the table. After one bite, Callie understood how Calhoun's had earned five stars. The syrupy blueberry sauce on her pork was tempered with just the right amount of peppery heat, while the meat was melt-in-your-mouth tender.

To a girl who had, more times than she could count, eaten cereal for dinner, it was absolute heaven, and she couldn't hold back a small moan of delight.

Across the table, Adam raised his eyebrows over amused eyes. "I gather you like it?"

"Love it," she said, around a bite.

After several silent forkfuls, she sat back, looking down at her half-eaten meal. She'd made good headway for someone with no appetite. Across from her, Adam cleaned his plate in silence, the rigid lines bracketing his mouth relaxing while his shoulders dipped. There they were again, sharing a meal at the kitchen table like a real married couple. Comfortable and cozy.

Except for the fact that someone had broken into their apartment a few hours before. That was about as cozy as a charging bear.

"What do we know?"

Adam appeared to pose the question more to the room at large than to her, but she answered anyway.

"We know the office was thoroughly searched but nothing was taken. I took inventory today and couldn't find so much as a single sticky note missing." A slight exaggeration, because she'd never actually counted their sticky notes, but it made her point.

"We know they were willing to bash you over the head, too," he said, pointing his fork in her direction.

"Don't remind me." She rubbed at the tender spot behind her ear.

"That's what concerns me the most," he continued. "Whatever they're looking for, they wanted it badly enough to clobber you for it." He twirled an impressive roll of pasta around his fork and popped it into his mouth.

"Yeah." She sighed. "I'm sorry, but I keep coming back to the Gutenberg. I mean, do you know for sure there's no truth to the story?"

His lips tightened. "For sure, no. How could I? I spoke with my grandfather about it earlier today and we agree it's family fiction. I mean, Gutenberg printed less than two hundred copies to begin with, and only about fifty are known to survive today." He shrugged. "I get that, to a collector of rare books, it would be the Holy Grail. But to find one here, in Virginia? That would be incredible."

She nodded. Hard to argue with that, but... "I'd pay to see the movie, though."

Their gazes locked, and they both burst out laughing. Belly laughing, like he had that night in her apartment, not just the polite chuckles they so often exchanged.

Callie's heart hummed with a happy buzz. What a crazy ending to a roller coaster of a day. There was no doubt about it. The universe was confusing as hell sometimes.

****

"So, you have no idea what it's all about?" Mason asked.

Tired to the bone, Adam switched the phone to his other ear and stretched out on his bed. "Do you?" he snapped.

"Hell, no. Not even a bad guess."

The good humor in his brother's voice amped up Adam's crankiness. "Hmph," he yawned. "Callie and I have a guess, but it's out there."

"How far out there?"

"What if someone's after the mythical Gutenberg?"

Mason's reaction was loud. So loud, Adam held the phone away from his ear for several seconds.

"Are you done?" he asked, once his brother's hysteria had died down.

"Maybe," Mason hedged, still chuckling. "I mean, c'mon. The Gutenberg? I'd sooner believe they're looking for proof you're a Martian."

"Ha-ha. Very funny. I'm serious. The story's gotten some traction from the press. Not on purpose, mind you. That article was supposed to be about my research on early manuscripts and the rise of…"

Exaggerated snoring noises came from the other end of the line. "Let me stop you right there. I admire your scholarship, but it's way beyond my feeble brain."

Adam laughed. Mason had graduated at the top of his class in med school. For all his laid-back, casual attitude, his little brother was hardly a slouch when it came to brain power. But Adam wasn't about to tell him that.

"You can say that again," he poked back. At Mason's pithy response, he added, "Nice. You owe Mum a hundred bucks."

Mason snorted. "Seriously, though. Both the house and grounds have been turned upside down a hundred times since the Civil War, without finding a single page, let alone a whole Bible."

Adam heard his sister-in-law's voice in the background, followed by his brother's laugh. "Priss thinks we should start digging holes all over the place, like in that movie." Mason said. "Can you imagine Mum's reaction?"

Adam shuddered. "She'd stroke out."

He stretched his free arm over his head and yawned again. The day's events and the lateness of the hour were beginning to take their toll. He should hang up and go to bed, but he needed to talk this whole thing through.

"But let's assume, just for the sake of argument, that someone believes the story to be true. Why target my office and apartment? By all accounts, the Bible if it exists, is hidden somewhere at Mum and Dad's."

Mason took a minute to answer. "I guess it's not that far-fetched. I mean, you're the historian of the family, and you're writing a book about ancient manuscripts, blah, blah, blah. It makes some sense that you'd be the keeper of a family Bible, Gutenberg, or no."

"Huh." Adam grabbed an extra pillow and crammed it behind his head. "If we had a Gutenberg, it would be in a museum."

"Yeah, *we'd* donate it to posterity, but there are plenty out there who wouldn't. There are a lot of collectors who pay small fortunes for illegally obtained artwork and artifacts, just for the thrill of having something they shouldn't. I read a whole article about it recently."

Adam laughed. "Reading the hospital's waiting room magazines again?"

"Best library in town." Mason's voice held a smile.

Priscilla said something Adam didn't catch again.

"I don't know, I'll ask," Mason said. "How'd they get up to the apartment, Adam?"

"They had a key card for the elevator."

Mason whistled. "You live in one of the safest buildings in the city. That, my friend, sounds like an inside job."

"That's what I said. I don't trust Bill Dobbs, the building's new chief of security, any farther than I can throw him." Adam pictured himself trying to toss the heavyset man; he worked out, but he wasn't *that* strong. "I just sent an email to that effect to the agent in charge. Dobbs was shocked by the second alarm. However, I'll say this much for him. If he's the one, he's sporting a brass pair. He was up here playing his role to the hilt."

"Interesting. This is starting to sound like a

sophisticated operation. Maybe the Gutenberg idea isn't so crazy after all."

"That's what scares me. In today's market, a Gutenberg is worth upwards of, I don't know, thirty-five million? Maybe more, to an illegal buyer. What if these break-ins are just the tip of the iceberg? What comes next?"

"I'm afraid to guess. But, for that kind of prize, chances are they're willing to keep trying. Did you alert the investigators to your treasure hunt theory?"

"I did, after I talked it over with Callie."

"Speaking of, how's she doing?"

Adam pictured his new wife, a mere two walls away. She was probably snuggled up in the guest room bed right now, those luscious curves of hers tucked into some filmy…

Flannel. With face cream all over her face. That was how he should be picturing Callie.

He adjusted his boxers and slid under the covers.

"She's okay. A little unnerved, but she's hanging in there." Which was more than he could say for himself. After the feds had left, he'd fought a crazy urge to sweep her up and whisk her off to a cave where she'd be safe. Talk about losing it.

"Good. You remember what Saturday is, right?"

Quickly, Adam counted the days in his head. With all that had happened lately, he'd lost track of the calendar. "Oh no. It's not Grandpa's eighty-fifth already?"

"Yep." Mason's voice held a warning. "And yes, you have to be there."

Adam risked his own one-hundred-dollar fine. "I assume it's at the farm?"

"Of course. Have you not been paying attention? That's the force behind Mum's big barn redo. You know she demo-ed everything, and the party's the big reveal. Everyone who's anyone will be there, including Angela."

Adam sighed. "God, I'd forgotten about Angela." And he hadn't missed her one little bit. She'd undoubtedly heard about his marriage by now and was plotting her next move. "She'll eat Callie alive."

"She'll try to, for sure. But my money's on Callie. She's tough."

"She is," Adam said, a little burst of pride warming his chest. "You should have seen her with the press tonight. We went to Jake's. I'm telling you, she had them eating out of the palm of her hand. Turns out she's a Paparazzi Whisperer."

Mason cheered. "Way to go, Callie! Sounds like your plan is working, although I reserve my right to say, 'I told you so,' if it all goes south. Speaking of going south, have you and your lovely wife done the nasty yet? Ouch! What was that for? You know you're wondering, too."

Adam frowned into phone. Leave it to Mason to bring the discussion around to the elephant in the room. Or, in his case, the elephant-sized erection. "I've told you before, smart ass. It's not that kind of relationship." *Could it be? Did he want it to be?*

"Methinks you doth protest too much."

Adam could hear the couple laughing again. "It's frightening to think you're a doctor. You have the emotional maturity of a twelve-year-old." On that fond note, Adam wished them both a good night and hung up.

Rolling to his side, he eyed the small photo sitting

on his bedside table. An unvarnished wood frame held an image of his younger self and Mallory, locked in a casual embrace. They were smiling at each other, frozen in time.

How very different his life was now. Since Mallory's death, he'd become a full professor, a successful author, and now he was husband to a new, convenient wife. It was a hell of a lot to swallow for a guy who loathed change.

Of course, once upon a time he hadn't liked broccoli either. Now, it was his favorite vegetable.

All he'd needed was one taste.

Chapter Eight

"You do realize I ought to kill you for this." Callie shot Adam her most severe stink eye while rearranging the fluffy folds of her dress for the fiftieth time.

For the hundredth time, she admired the long length of tuxedoed male sitting next to her. Talk about a teenage dream.

He gave a low chuckle. "I've already apologized for giving you a mere *four days* to get ready. Now, stop fussing. You look…beautiful."

Flustered by the whispered last word, she let her hand fall back onto the limo's bench seat and turned toward the window. She was just in time to catch sight of the magnificent Lincoln Memorial. Its iconic white marble columns—thirty-six of them, one for each state in Lincoln's reunited Union—gleamed ethereally in the waning evening light, while "Honest Abe" sat within.

"I love this town."

She was unaware she'd spoken aloud until Adam agreed. "It's the best city on earth." Twisting, she turned to face him, and he gave her a sheepish grin. "Of course, as a native, I'm biased."

She laughed. "True, but you mean it, don't you?"

"Every word. I can't imagine living anywhere else. Where did you grow up?"

Unbidden and unwanted memories swamped her, taking her back to the cramped, dingy apartment where she and Gretchen had been raised. Before the accident changed everything. "Baltimore."

His eyes narrowed. "You said that like it's a bad word."

She managed a bitter grin. Theirs had been a dismal childhood, but that had nothing to do with her hometown. "It isn't Baltimore's fault," she admitted at last, burrowing her hands in her lap. "Truth is, my parents would have made a mess of things no matter where they lived, as long as they had access to a liquor store."

Her breath caught in her throat, and she coughed to clear it. She hadn't meant to say that.

Adam withdrew an inch or two, though whether in surprise or disgust, she couldn't guess. "Your parents drank a lot?"

No use denying it now. "Um…yes. They were both alcoholics."

"I'm sorry. That must have been tough."

Shrugging, she returned to her window-gazing. "We didn't know the difference."

That, of course, was a colossal lie. They'd noticed other children's parents made wholesome breakfasts and lunches, saw their children off to school, and showed up at school events as promised, all without reeking of alcohol. They'd also noticed other parents didn't sleep off benders on the living room floor or spend their children's field trip money on brown-bagged bottles.

Yet all of that paled in comparison to the endless fighting. Her parents' constant bickering and the occasional well-placed punch or tossed china had made their daughters' lives a living hell.

Adam cleared his throat. "The accident…your hip. Was one of your parents responsible?"

She winced but didn't duck it. Chances were good he wouldn't connect any dots. "Yeah. My dad. He and my mother weren't wearing seatbelts, and they died on impact." The memory was old, but it still stung. She fingered the jagged ridge of the scar on her cheek.

The scenery switched from gray city sidewalks to the fading green lawns of suburban Virginia. Soon, they'd reach his parents' farm. She gulped down a swallow and bent to fiddle with her beautiful new shoes.

"My late wife, Mallory, was killed by a drunk driver."

Adam's words, spoken in the raw, froze Callie to the spot. Never before had he spoken of this. She wet her lips. "I know. I'm sorry."

The limo's sound system piped in some smooth jazz, but it hardly registered over the throb of blood rushing in her ears. She glanced over at Adam. Now he was the one taking an excessive interest in their surroundings.

What a pair they made.

Straightening, she tugged on her shoulder belt, taking solace in its tightness, before her hands fell idle once more. Her breath caught again as Adam, moving in slow motion, laced their fingers together.

Callie couldn't say whether twenty minutes passed or two. A paralyzing battle raged inside her. One side—the sensible side, led by her head—sounded a loud retreat, but the reckless, heart-strong part of her damned the torpedoes, ready to jump headlong into a real relationship with the man who was now her husband.

The man whose late wife's death hung, like a lead weight, around her heart.

She unthreaded her fingers from his as they turned into the long gravel driveway leading to his parents' house.

"I really should kill you," she repeated as the cab slowed, then stopped altogether for the crowd of reporters waiting outside the property's open entry gate. The group might have been hesitant to trespass, but that didn't stop them from surrounding the car.

"I do owe you one," Adam conceded, meeting her eyes with his own. The shadows had lifted. The moment of mutual pain and understanding had passed, and they were back on a lighter footing.

She cocked an eyebrow. "You're pretty calm considering fifty photojournalists are snapping your picture right now."

He leaned toward her, and she caught a whiff of pine-scented shampoo and spicy aftershave. "I've decided to take a page out of your book. If you can't beat 'em…"

Smiling, she gave him two thumbs-up. "Good for you."

His answering smile reached his eyes, kicking her pulse up a notch. What was so amusing?

"Want to give them a show?" With smooth expertise, he slid his arm around her waist and tugged her close. When his mouth was a mere inch from hers, he paused, hovering, questioning, waiting.

All she had to do was pull away. Both his eyes and his hands told her he would let her go if that was what she wanted.

It wasn't. Not by half. Deep in her core, the ember of desire that only he fanned, burst into flame.

There were nine hundred reasons this was a bad idea, and she ignored every one of them. Instead, she slid her hands up the unyielding hardness of his chest.

Gripping the woven cloth of his jacket lapels, she urged him forward until their mouths met, warm and wet and hungry.

His lips claimed hers with a soft but unyielding pressure, a hint of tongue and teeth, and a thoroughness that blew her mind. *Good God.* This could become addictive.

And then—the moment was gone.

He drew back and, calm as the proverbial cucumber, gave the driver directions as they threaded their way past the paparazzi, through the gate, and on up the long drive.

Callie sank back in her seat, staring straight ahead. For years, she had fought her attraction to this man, certain beyond a doubt that if she gave in to it, even for a second, she would be lost.

She'd never been more right about anything.

****

The long ripples of Callie's hair swayed against her back as she laughed at something Justice Holloway said. The judge was one of Adam's father's more austere colleagues, but after five minutes of conversation with Callie, the man was clearly besotted.

Not a big surprise. She was, like his mother, the same person in public she was in private, and authenticity was rare in this town. No one remained immune to his new wife's open, honest, caring personality for long.

Speaking of honesty, Adam mentally kicked himself. He was a Class-A idiot. He shouldn't have touched her, let alone pressed his lips against hers in a kiss that shot him into the stratosphere. The memory alone had his body tensing in ways best avoided in public places.

"Lovely party as always, Adam darling."

He clenched his fists. That low-pitched hiss belonged to the one person he'd been hoping to avoid. But it was his grandfather's birthday, a family celebration. He'd play nice.

Forcing a fake smile, he turned around. "Angela."

With a speed Hussein Bolt would envy, Angela Carson laced her hands around his neck and tugged him down for a kiss that, despite his attempts to turn away, still landed half on, half off his mouth.

The move was vintage Angela. A bit on the naughty side, but not so much it would raise any eyebrows except his own. He wiped off any traces of her hot pink lipstick with his cocktail napkin and tried to keep his expression neutral.

"Hello, I don't think we've met. I'm Callie, Adam's wife." Presto, change-o. As if he'd conjured her up, Callie stepped in front of him.

A juvenile sense of victory went through him when he noted how Callie's tall, curvy frame towered over Angela's diminutive, stick-insect one. Adam set a hand on his wife's good hip, hoping the stance conveyed both intimacy and solidarity.

Angela waved Callie off. "I know who you are." She fluttered her fake eyelashes at Adam. "Aren't you the sneaky one."

She spoke in a rehearsed imitation of the way Marilyn Monroe had once wished JFK a happy birthday. Adam had fallen for that act once, a million years ago, but now he saw it for what it was. A way to entrap the poor SOBs of the world. The *rich* SOBs. Angela had the highest standards when it came to bank accounts. However, her standards were drastically lower in most other departments.

"I don't know what you mean." *Don't lose your temper. She isn't worth it.*

Angela gave him a playful little pout and pushed her professionally coiffed titian hair back behind an ear accented by a cool, two-karat diamond stud. Hollywood perfection. Symmetrical features, perfect teeth, hard body she worked on with a trainer every day. Oh, yes, Angela could stop traffic.

But behind all the glamour, she was as warm as a day in the Arctic and ruthless to go with it.

"I read about your marriage, darling, and I have four words for you: I'm not buying it."

Before he could muster a retort, Callie laughed. Either her amusement was genuine, or she was a better actress than he thought. "You misunderstand. We're not selling anything. It's been very entertaining, watching you chase after Adam this past year, but now that we've put a ring on it, I'm afraid it's 'game over.'" Callie's voice was quiet but firm, her body taut.

His fingers itched to make a foray upward, along her ribcage, but he held still, waiting to see what came next. She was giving out a decided "don't push me or we'll take this outside" vibe that was both impressive and one hell of a turn-on.

Angela's right eye twitched ever so slightly. Callie had scored a hit. However, Angela never went down without a fight.

"Puh-lease." She set her hands on her hips and looked at Callie the same way she might look at a bug. "I never heard of you until two weeks ago. Something's up. I don't know how you trapped him into this marriage, but make no mistake, you won't stop us from being together."

Adam ground his teeth with such force, he worried he might dislocate his jaw. Bill Dobbs had been ballsy, but the man had nothing on this scheming little bitch. He wrapped his arms around Callie, linking his fingers together against the flatness of her stomach as she leaned back against his chest.

As a protective gesture, it backfired, big time. Now her sweet little ass was in line with his crotch; one more tempting little inch and she'd be nestled tight against him. Angela stirred his anger, but Callie stirred something else entirely.

"I took vows, Angela, and I intend to keep them," he said.

Angela raised her heavily penciled brows. "My, my. I guess I've been warned, haven't I?"

Callie crossed her arms, running her hands along his forearms. They were fully entwined now, which should have all his intimacy alarms blaring, yet he had no desire to bolt. Was he losing his edge? He couldn't blame it on alcohol since he had yet to drink a drop. That might soon change.

"I hate to break this to you, Angela." Callie's tone implied no such thing. "You've got about as much chance now as you had this past summer."

Angela's eyes narrowed. "What are you talking about?"

"Adam and I aren't quite the 'new item' you think we are." Callie glanced up at him, wearing the same come-hither expression she'd donned for the photogs at Calhoun's. He fought an urge to kiss her right then and there.

Where was that picture of Jeep's dog?

"I was with him at the cabin," Callie continued. "Your attempts to catch him then didn't work, and they won't now."

Surprise flickered in the depths of Angela's dark brown eyes. "You were there?"

It was as natural as breathing for him to lean down and nuzzle Callie's neck. God, her skin was soft. "Yes. Cal's been by my side for quite a few years."

Bam! Another hit scored. If Angela wasn't such a snake, he'd almost feel sorry for her.

"Well, well, well." Angela sent a royal wave to someone across the room before levelling a poisonous look at Callie. "Fine. Enjoy him while you can. I've told everyone he's mine, and he will be. Eventually, he'll tire of hamburger and come looking for a filet with plenty of sizzle." She lifted her gaze to his. "And when you do, you know right where to find me."

With that, she slipped away, her manicured claws fluttering as she zeroed in on a society matron across the room.

Adam heaved a heavy sigh of relief. Any Angela encounter that ended without dead bodies strewn about was a lucky one.

"Wow!" Callie stepped out of his embrace and chewed on her lip a second. "I've never been so mean in my life. But that's what you wanted, right?"

"Yes. Don't be fooled. That is one dangerous woman," he warned, taking her elbow, and leading her toward the loaded buffets.

"Hmm. Social scheming dangerous or hit-over-the-head dangerous?"

He paused. Angela wouldn't. Would she?

"I think just social scheming." He was ninety-nine-point-nine percent sure, but he'd keep an eye on Angela anyway. Picking up a warm plate, he replayed the scene in his head. "You were brilliant, by the way. That part about the cabin? Pure genius. How'd you think of it?"

Callie handed him a bundle of silverware rolled in a cloth napkin and grabbed one for herself. "Yeah, well… Again, I'm not super proud of it. I saw the society photos of her at your cabin this summer and remembered you said the untold story was that you turned her away flat, without letting her step foot inside. I imagined what would make me jealous and went for it."

He was a little intrigued by the idea of a jealous Callie. "I think it worked, at least for now," he said, helping himself to some Caesar salad. "I certainly wouldn't waste time feeling bad about it. Like I said, she's a snake, through and through."

Callie spooned some tabbouleh onto her plate before following him to the larger table filled with main courses. "She's certainly determined to get you. What's that all about? I mean, sure, you're a catch and all, but…"

His ego perked up at her words. She considered him a catch? He couldn't hold back a grin.

"I'm off the market, remember?" The smell of roast beef and his mother's special chicken piccata made his mouth water. "I suspect she's after the part of the femme fatale in the next Wolfe Bridges movie."

Light dawned in Callie's eyes. "Ohhh, gotcha. She thinks she'll have a better shot if she's your girlfriend."

His ears tingled as he filled his plate. "Yeah. Mainly, she's just trying to be seen with me. That's what the whole farce at the cabin was about. For all her talk, she's more about being caught at the right time at the right place and parlaying that into what she wants. I'm sure she posed for the press at the gate tonight. But, enough about her."

Callie scanned the room. "This is quite a party! I've never met so many people before in my life. It's kinda…" She left the sentence unfinished with a shrug.

"Exhausting," he said, flatly. "Boring. Inane."

Her laughter treated him to a great view of the creamy expanse of her neck. "It's not that bad. Look at all this food! My plate weighs twenty pounds."

He took her elbow again, steering her through the crowd. "Tell you what. Let's play hooky for a little while. There are so many people here right now, no one will know we're gone."

She hesitated, biting her lip. "I'd love to, but I don't want to upset your parents."

Hypnotized, he couldn't take his eyes from her lips. Lips he was now intimately familiar with and, damn it, wanted to know better.

Those lips lifted into a smile and parted to show even white teeth. "But I must admit, I could use a break. Let's make a run for it."

He laughed. "That's the spirit."

"One sec." She dropped a cookie on both her own plate and his. That was another thing he appreciated about Callie; she ate real food like a real person.

Adam led the way through the crowded room to one of the open, garage-style glass doors lining one side of the rehabbed barn. It was a moonless but starry night. He couldn't hear the roll of the river over the noise of the party, but this was his home turf. He could find his way around blindfolded and walking backward.

"Wait. I can't see. Where are we going?" Callie said as they left the patio.

He grabbed her free hand. Her fingers were cool, and she shivered in the crisp breeze rising from the river. Without thinking, he tucked their entwined hands into his jacket pocket and instantly regretted the move. He'd already kissed her and embraced her tonight, maybe or maybe not just for show, and that almost maxed out his self-control.

For all that, however, he couldn't quite make himself release her. "It's not far, I promise. It's one of my favorite places here on the farm."

Adjusting his stride to hers, he guided her to the narrow pea-gravel path that sloped down toward the Potomac. The lapping sounds of river against shore grew louder as they neared the dock. "Okay. Careful, there are steps here. That's it."

"A boathouse! You aren't planning on going out on the water, are you? I don't think we should be gone that long."

"No. We won't be." Letting go of her hand, he felt along the top of one of the old, lead-paned windows, located the key his parents should have removed long ago, and opened the door.

The rush of stale, musty air blew him straight back to childhood. As a kid, he'd traded the bustling activities of the main house for the cool calm of the unused building whenever he could.

He flipped on the lights, illuminating the empty docks and the narrow, twisty stairway leading up to the second floor. "This has never been used in my lifetime, except as storage. Gramps built a bigger boathouse upriver, sometime in the mid-1950s, after he returned from Korea."

"Let me guess—your mother plans on turning this

into a guest house, or offices or something," Callie said with a grin.

Adam chuckled. That sounded like something his mum would do. "Without a doubt, although I think her next project is turning the old blacksmith's forge into some kind of barbeque. She's been so busy building her business, she hasn't had time to do anything with the outbuildings before now."

"Not to mention raising you and your brothers," Callie added.

"Yeah, that too. Not an easy feat." He grinned. "We were hellions."

She rolled her eyes. "I can imagine."

They shared a laugh that trailed into a slight awkwardness. Why had he brought her down there? They'd been just fine at the party, surrounded by three hundred of his grandfather's friends.

He cleared his throat and raised his full plate. "Let's go eat." Worry hit him as he approached the old staircase. It looked steeper than he remembered. "Can you manage the steps?"

"I'll be fine," she said sharply, then chuckled. "There I go again, getting all defensive when you're just being nice. Thank you for your concern, but my hip feels pretty good tonight. I hate to admit it, but that guestroom mattress of yours has helped."

"Good. After you." Averting his mind from Callie-plus-bed-equals-sexy, and his gaze from her sweet little behind, he gave her a good head start.

The second floor was just as he remembered. Cobwebbed, dusty, and filled with all manner of junk.

"Oh. My. Gosh. I'm in heaven!" Callie turned in a circle, eyes wide. "Look at all this stuff. Oh, my gosh, this table." She ran a hand down the dusty wood of a library table that took up two-thirds of the room. "Adam! This would look amazing in your dining room. So much more welcoming than that glass-topped monstros—" Her voice faded as she clapped a hand over her mouth. "Sorry," she said, against her hand. Lowering it, she gave him a chagrined smile. "I shouldn't have said that. It's your house, and it's just the way you like it. Can we strike that from the record?"

Her excitement over the antiques was so sincere, he took no offense. "It's your house, too." He drew a finger over the tabletop and wrote out "clean me" in the dust. "I used to do my homework here. With Mason and Jeep around, it was one of the few places I found any peace." His gaze ran the length of the well-worn, solidly built piece. "You might be right. It's a better size—much better than my glass monstrosity," he teased. "Let's test it out."

He set his plate down on the scarred surface and freed an ancient but sound ladder-backed chair from under a long-forgotten picnic basket. After dusting it off with his linen napkin, he waved her into it. "Milady."

She sat, spine straight, nose in the air. "Thank you, James." Then she giggled. "Isn't that what butlers are always called?"

Joining in her laughter, he hooked a three-legged stool with his foot and sat himself. "Works for me. Maybe I'll make a butler named 'James' the bad guy in the next Bridges book. That way—"

"The butler could do it," they finished in unison.

For a few minutes, they ate in companionable silence, the only noise the soft "swish, swish" of the river below. Yet another thing he liked about Callie. She didn't need to always be talking.

"So, what are your parents planning to do with all this junk-slash-treasure?" she asked, once they'd both made serious headway on their dinners.

Adam finished chewing a bite of his salad and used his napkin before answering. Caesar dressing wouldn't go well with his tuxedo.

"I've no idea. Nor do they. All this crap has been here longer than I have." He laughed again, this time at her bug-eyed look. "I mean it. If you see anything else you like, chances are it's up for grabs."

"You don't have to tell me twice." Leaving her plate half-finished, she pushed back her chair and wandered over to an ancient, pigeonhole desk.

One by one, she set aside a ripped lampshade, a chipped china teapot, and another decaying picnic basket, until the ancient piece stood alone.

"This is an old clerk's desk," she said, an awestruck expression on her face. "I bet this is from the early 1800s, at least." She fingered the wooden filigree. "If your parents don't want it, and I mean, *really* don't want it, then I'd love to borrow it. Just while we're married, of course."

"No, ma'am," he argued. "If it's free to a good home like I think it is, it's yours to keep." He raised a hand as she began to protest. "I'm speaking for my parents, too. Trust me, Dad will be overjoyed to see something leaving the place."

"Okay."

He watched as embarrassment overtook her excitement. *Charming.*

"I'd offer to pay you, but considering I already owe you a ridiculous amount of money, that would be kind of absurd."

"You don't owe me anything," he said, putting truth in every word. "We have a deal that benefits us both, and you worked hard tonight. Angela aside, simply braving Justice Martinez makes you a hero in my book."

Callie tsked at him. "That's an awful thing to say. She's a very sweet old woman."

He grinned. "You might not think so if you'd grown up around her."

After a few tugs, she managed to pull the desk's large center drawer open. "She was telling me about her granddaughter." Her nose crinkled as she glanced his way. "Sounded like she was hoping to do a little matchmaking, before we got married."

Adam pushed his empty plate aside and slid off the stool, stretching. "Yeah, that was never going to happen. No spark whatsoever. Plus, Lucy's been seeing the same guy for years. He's been a little slow to propose, so the judge thought she'd dangle me in front of the guy to move things along."

"Hmm." Callie blew into one of the desk's pigeonholes before sticking her hand inside. "Well," she sent him a laughing glance, "we wouldn't want you dangling, that's for sure. Huh…" Withdrawing her hand, she bent down to examine the hole more closely. "There's something in here."

"Not a black widow," he said, not entirely in jest.

She frowned and reached in again. "No, it's a piece of paper. I can't quite get it." With a grunt, she stretched until her arm was buried well past her elbow. "Got it."

Straightening, she withdrew a folded, age-stained envelope and brought it over to the table.

Adam stared down at it, half expecting it to bite.

Then the historian in him woke up. The note looked authentically ancient. "Aren't you going to open it?" he asked.

Callie's gaze remained glued to the envelope also. "Nope. The desk belongs to your family, so it's your note."

He made a face, then opened the flap, and withdrew several folded sheets of paper. The writing was sloped and spidery, the paper thin and torn along one edge. It was peppered with random splotches of ink, as if written in haste with a leaky pen. He scanned a few lines.

"Holy shit!" He fumbled around with the sheets. "I think these are pages torn from my great-great-great-great-grandfather's diary. Gramps showed it to me several years ago, but there were pages missing." He pointed to the right-hand corner. "*December 14, 1862.* Good Lord. That was during the Battle of Fredericksburg. A Confederate victory," he added, at her questioning look. "Listen to this: *Burnside overwhelmed. We prepare to abandon the farm. I fear I shall never lay eyes on it again. German Bible hidden in safe place. Don't dare take it or much else. Below, B/Ds.*"

He spread the pages out on the table. "It's a list of births and deaths."

Callie reached out as if to touch the paper, then yanked her hand back. "Look at the dates! *1457, 1458, 1462*…it goes on and on. And the names. *Johann, Greta, Karl*…Adam, it's incredible."

Adrenaline surged through his body as the document's importance sank in, leaving him zinging from head to foot. He grasped Callie's elbows, craving the physical connection. "Do you know what this means?"

She grabbed his arms right back. "I'm not sure. Do I?"

"The Gutenberg Bibles were printed right around 1455, right?"

"Yes, they were the first to be printed, on Gutenberg's press. That's why they're so valuable."

"Exactly. These entries were copied out of a *German Bible*, and the first name listed is a birth from 1457."

"So, you're saying…" Her eyes bored into his, as if daring him to go ahead and say it.

"I'm saying, Gutenberg was German, and the only copies of the Bible that existed outside of churches in 1457 *were—*"

"The ones he printed." Her grip tightened around his elbows. "Adam, the family legend might be true!"

"It might." Throwing his head back, he laughed at the impossible possibility of it all.

"Oh. My. Gosh." With a breathy cry, Callie launched herself into his arms.

He couldn't say what excited him more, their amazing discovery or the press of her curves against his angles.

Either way, it was turning into one helluva party.

Chapter Nine

For the second time in as many months, Callie woke to the sound of banging. Swimming to the surface after another amazing night's sleep—seriously, she needed to ask Adam to add this mattress to their marriage contract—she attempted to focus her decaffeinated mind on where the persistent noise was coming from.

Not her room anyway, a sleepy but satisfied glance confirmed. The sunshine-filled room was a far cry from the austere guest room she'd walked into six long weeks ago. A weekend with a paintbrush had changed the bluish-white walls to a cheerful canary yellow. A little over a week ago, much to her delight, Adam had brought the old clerk's desk from the farm and set it in one corner. Her signature pink, orange, and yellow patterned pillows had made the trek uptown from her apartment, and the new turquoise throw she'd knitted was so wonderfully soft she couldn't stop petting it.

With Minna and Patrick's blessings, Callie had also rescued several other items from the boathouse, including an old dress form, a few elderly botanical prints, and a 1952 wire-bound calendar that proudly advertised "Peak's Fishing Gear—The Peak of Every Season." In short, the room was now an eclectic mix of old and new, rusty and shiny, practical and whimsical.

Heaven.

But she was wasting daylight and was curious to know what all the noise was about. After pairing her favorite pair of leggings with an oversized thrifted sweatshirt from a college she'd never heard of, she battled with her hair. By now, the banging was less frequent, and her hair was metaphorically giving her the finger, so she abandoned the brush and gave in to her curiosity.

"Ouch! Careful. That was my thumb, dickhead." Jeep's deep voice carried from the dining room.

"Then move your thumb, dumb ass," Adam's baritone snapped back.

"These terms of endearment are touch—" Her sarcasm trailed off as she entered the room. There, in all its glory, stood the old library table from Adam's parents' boathouse.

"Oh, my gosh!" She stared at Adam for a long moment, searching for the right words. "You moved it."

Way to go, Captain Obvious.

"*We* moved it," Mason clarified as he entered from the kitchen, chewing on a ham sandwich. "I hope you like it because it's not going anywhere. It weighs a bloody ton."

Jeep scoffed. "How would you know? Adam and I carried the damn thing. All you did was follow along, barking orders."

Mason smirked and raised his sandwich. "I was supervising."

Ignoring all the brotherly love zinging around her, Callie stepped over to the table, thrilled with how the grain of the wood glinted gold in the sunlight. The antique gave the dining room a welcoming warmth its predecessor had lacked.

"It's perfect. I love it!" She met Adam's eyes with some trepidation. "What do you think?"

They'd been roommates now for nearly two months, but she still thought of the place as his, and if he didn't like the table, its days were numbered.

He stepped back and took a long look, then shook his head. "It looks like it was made to go here. I don't know how you do it, but you have a gift for giving discarded things new life."

Their eyes met over the glowing wood, her body humming at both his warm expression and the unexpected compliment. Nothing he might have said could have pleased her more.

"Ahem. Would you two like a little privacy?"

Heat flooded her cheeks as Mason's words jerked her out of her trance.

Adam glared at him. "Ever since you got married, you've had a one-track mind."

Mason grinned, like a pigeon-eating cat. "Damn straight."

"I have to admit, it does look good," Jeep said, circling the table. "Much better than that ugly-ass thing you had before."

"Okay, okay. I agree. The old table sucked," Adam broke in, laughing. He waved a hand toward the kitchen and living room. "Have at it, Callie. The apartment is yours. Change anything you want."

This was too good to be true. "Are you serious?"

He gave her the full wattage of one of his smiles, kicking her already elevated heart rate up another notch.

"I am." He glanced at his brothers. "We're headed back to Mum and Dad's to search the old kitchen. It's not much more than a pile of rubble now, but if that Bible is still on the farm somewhere, we're going to find it. Want to tag along? We can pick up Gretchen on the way, if you'd like," he continued before she could quash his offer with her usual excuse. "I promised I'd teach her how to feed the chickens. While we're busy, you can prowl around and see if there's any other old furniture that sets your Spidey senses tingling."

For a moment, Callie wondered what he'd do if she told him *he* set her senses tingling. Probably pass out right here, bumping his head on the table on his way down.

"Sure, I guess. I-I mean, that would be great." She bit her tongue.

What was she? A teenager? Only Adam could reduce her to a stammering mess with one smile and an invite to the farm. It was tempting fate to agree to being within twenty miles of his sexy self, outside the protection of the office, but she loved searching for vintage finds. She'd just have to keep her libido in lockdown.

A picture of heavy metal chains and a large padlock came to mind. *Yep. That should do it. Problem solved.*

She sighed. If only it was that easy.

"There's still a shi—" With a sheepish grin, Mason edited himself, "shiny shirt's worth of stuff in the boathouse and the old tobacco barn."

"There's another barn?" Callie asked, as Jeep fired a finger gun toward his youngest brother, in obvious appreciation of Mason's alliteration.

"Yep. It's even older than the one Mum converted. I'm talking George Washington old and piled to the rafters with God-knows-what. It was always off-limits to us as kids," Mason added.

"Yeah, because Dad was afraid some of the shit would fall over and kill us." They all laughed at Jeep's comment and his customary lack of editing.

"You two can head back," Adam told Mason. "Callie and I will be right behind you after a good breakfast. And by that, I don't mean a ham sandwich." He looked pointedly at the crusty remains in Mason's fingers.

With a shrug, his brother finished the last bite. "I was at the hospital until oh-dark-thirty last night, and my stomach lost track of the time," he said, defensively. "Any time is sandwich time, in my book."

Jeep shivered. "Ugh. Dijon mustard before ten a.m.? No, thank you." He turned to Callie. "Uh, will Eloise be coming with your sister?" His massive shoulders rose and fell. "Not that it matters. I just wondered if she read a book I recommended."

Hmm. Was it just a trick of the light, or were the big, macho, former Navy SEAL's ears turning red? *Interesting.*

But before Callie summoned her matchmaking mojo, the brothers were on the move. With their plans now set, Mason and Jeep gathered the tools they'd brought along and headed for the elevator.

"If we find that Bible before you get there, we're taking full credit for it," Mason warned Adam.

"And if we find any attractive rocks or dead bugs, we'll save them for you." Jeep gave her a wink as he stepped into the waiting elevator. "You know, in case you want to pretty them up and put them on display, too."

Callie laughed as the doors slid shut, a little scared at how quickly she'd embraced the easy-going banter that was the heart of any Hughes family conversation. It was alien to her, this warm, loving, functional family unit. She'd do well to remember that this whole situation was temporary.

Problem was, they were just so damn...*likable*.

Their acceptance of her—not to mention her sister—was bulldozing her self-reliance. Every time she turned around, someone from the freaking family was doing something nice. Callie had come home the other day to find her mother-in-law had left a five-course "test" meal in their fridge that she was experimenting with for her show. *Five* courses!

Patrick had called the other day just to "check in," and, of course, despite the differences in their personalities, both her brothers-in-law were total sweethearts. She hadn't spent much time with Mason's wife, Priscilla, but from what she'd seen, the woman was every bit as thoughtful as the rest of the Hughes clan. Taken as a group, they were more than a little intimidating, yet Callie couldn't quite stay away.

They were reeling her in, bit by bit.

Then there was her husband, who, she'd discovered, excelled at the small things as well as the big ones. For example, when he'd learned she made a habit of skipping breakfast, he'd insisted on fixing a hot meal for her every day. Pancakes, French toast, eggs. She'd never had it so good. To him, it was no big deal, but to a girl who'd grown up eating dry cereal straight out of the box, it struck a chord with the force of a nuclear bomb.

But more precious than the food, during those private moments at the breakfast table, *they talked!* From gardening to current events to whether brown should be a color, they'd covered it all. It was intoxicating to relate to another person so well.

Intoxicating and dangerous. She could fall for this man in a big, never-coming-back-from-it way.

And that would be the worst mistake of her life.

****

The car's tires protested as Adam grazed some of the gravel along the berm. He rarely took the SUV out anymore, but he was in a mood to drive this morning. Maybe he had a need to control something since, these days, his personal life appeared to have a mind of its own. Without question, he needed to get his head out of his pants.

Sure, it had been a long time, but… every time he looked at Callie, *bam*! His long-dormant sex drive reminded him he wasn't dead yet.

Nothing he and a few dozen cold showers couldn't handle.

Like his dad, he was a thinker. Maybe it was the natural by-product of being raised by a jurist, but he believed actions were best undertaken only after careful deliberation. But when it came to Callie, every brain cell he'd ever possessed fled like elephants before an earthquake.

Worst of all, he wasn't sure he *wanted* to think anymore, at least where she was concerned. For the first time in his life, he was flirting with the idea of acting first and thinking later. Letting, as his grandfather was fond of saying, the chips fall where they may. Following his nose. Or to be completely honest, another part of his anatomy altogether.

Even before he'd met Mallory, he hadn't been one for casual hookups. Angela had been his first real relationship and, while he wasn't proud of it in hindsight, she'd sunk her claws in deep. It had drawn a fair amount of blood when she'd dumped him for the Hollywood playboy she'd been seeing on the side.

Soon after that breakup, Mallory had arrived on the scene and managed, albeit with a fair amount of work, to wrangle her way into his bruised heart. Once she'd proven he could trust her unconditionally, he'd never looked back.

Which brought him to Callie.

She forced him outside his comfort zone, in more ways than one. Yes, she'd invaded his inner sanctum. That was part but not all of it. After years of marriage, his relationship with Mal had been cozy and, dare he say it? Predictable, but in the best, most wonderful sense of the word. Callie, on the other hand, set him off-kilter. He was two-wheeling it where he was used to having all four wheels glued to the good old terra firma. And the excitement that thrummed through him when he was with her wasn't just sexual.

The bottom line was, he should be staying the hell away from her, not inviting her to share the day with him. Yet every damn time he opened his mouth, he came up with another excuse to stay in her company. He enjoyed being with her, making her laugh, hearing her opinions. And then there was that kiss…

That kiss made him wonder, what if he just gave in to temptation? He was pretty sure the attraction was mutual, so, why not?

"I don't know. Do they, Adam?"

The external question trumped his internal ones. "What? Sorry, I was thinking about something else." *Like how incredible we'd be together.*

"Do chickens bite?"

The difference between his own thoughts and Gretchen's question made him laugh. He gave his sister-in-law a brief glance in the rearview mirror. "Yes, definitely." He lifted a hand from the steering wheel. "I have the scars to prove it. They'll peck at you with their beaks if you're not paying attention, so you have to be on your guard when you're gathering eggs. That said, my mother's raised all these hens herself, with a lot of TLC. They're her babies, and they're pretty well-behaved."

"Are you sure it's safe?" From the other end of the backseat, the hitch in Eloise's voice revealed her nerves. "I'm a city girl. All I know about chickens is that they taste good."

"I'm with you, El." Buckled beside him, Callie switched her worried gaze from her sister to him. "Maybe we should take a pass on the chickens."

Adam laughed again. "I've been feeding them since I could walk. You'll be fine, Gretchen," he assured her. "The goats are the ones to watch out for. If you're not careful, they'll give you a little love bite in the butt."

Gretchen giggled.

"Is there anything your mother can't do?" Callie asked, with a smile. "She's incredible. Was she raised on a farm?"

"Nope. She's also a city girl, grew up in one of the London suburbs, surrounded by pavement. But she's always had a passion for growing and making and cooking. When she first started the show, the challenge was to modernize the things she loved which, at the time, were being dismissed as old-fashioned and out-of-line with the women's movement, etcetera. She didn't see them that way, and she fought to bring them back into the mainstream. It was and is her belief that people can balance their careers with creative lives at home if the tasks they take on are vetted and quick."

"You're very proud of her."

There was a ring of surprise in her voice, and Adam wondered if she was thinking about her own mother, whose talents and eventually her life, had been lost to a disease she couldn't beat.

"I am proud. She began doing this long before the internet and social media, and it was an uphill climb. And no, there isn't anything she won't try. To Dad's dismay, she once spent weeks taking her car apart, then putting it back together again, because she felt people—women, in particular—should know more about auto repair."

From the backseat, Eloise made an approving sound. "She's got that right. I don't know one end of a dipstick from another."

This launched Gretchen into several questions about cars. While Eloise did her best to answer those, Callie whispered her own question about the Gutenberg search.

"It's early days. We've got over fifty-five acres to search, and we don't know if it's underground or above." Adam kept his voice down, too. He doubted Gretchen or Eloise would repeat whatever they might overhear, but at this point, they couldn't be too careful. "We're starting with any building we know existed in 1862. That includes the old boathouse, which came up empty, the old kitchen, the tobacco barn—which you'll see is both huge and a colossal mess—the carriage house, the horse barn, the forge, and a good part of the main house."

"Geez, that is a lot of ground to cover. At our wedding lunch, your grandfather told me the farm once stretched throughout most of the county. There's no way you can search the entire area, is there?"

"No, but most of it has gone through a great deal of development over the past hundred years, and nothing has turned up. Based on the note you found, I think the

Bible's hidden somewhere on the main part of the property. That's *if* it exists at all."

Callie shifted in the black leather seat, and he caught a whiff of the citrusy shampoo she used. "Don't you think, given the note we found, that it does?" she asked.

Adam hesitated. The scholar in him was conflicted. On one hand, it would be an amazing find. On the other, the odds of it surviving, without years of careful preservation, were next to zero.

"Yes and no," he said, hedging. "It's obvious there was an old family Bible. It's even plausible, based on the dates we found, that the Bible was a Gutenberg. But for it to have gone undiscovered for so long…" He rolled his shoulders and tried to unkink his neck. "I honestly don't know what to think."

"Hey, Adam," Gretchen said. "Why do you write the wrong kind of books?"

Chuckling, he shot Callie a questioning glance. "The *wrong* kind of books?"

Her freckles danced as twin pink spots appeared on her cheeks. "Let me explain. A long time ago, she wanted me to read her one of your books, and I told her it was the wrong kind of story. A little too, um, spicy, if you know what I mean. She's never forgotten."

"Fair enough. So, what do you think I should write about, Gretchen?"

His sister-in-law was silent for a moment. "How about a story about a girl named Gretchen who lives on a farm and feeds chickens and plays with goats!"

Beside him, Callie hid a laugh by chewing on her luscious upper lip, instantly derailing his thoughts onto a more intimate track.

Nope. Not now. Children's fiction. Chickens and

goats.

"That sounds like a good story." He nodded into the rearview mirror.

"And Callie could draw the pictures," Gretchen suggested.

Adam glanced at his wife again, eyebrows raised. "You can draw?"

Man. It was pathetic how little he knew about this woman he'd worked beside for the past five years. Had he been buried under a rock?

Yes. Yes, he had. A large rock with the words "Defensive Lonely Asshole Lives Here" scrawled across the top.

She waved a hand. "I doodle a little, that's all."

"She went to school for it and everything. Until she got hurt." Straining against her seatbelt, Gretchen cheerfully provided the details Callie had left out.

"You did? Why are you working for me, then? You should be out pursuing your art."

Callie waved a hand. "Sure. It's totally that easy. I live in the real world, remember? With bills and rent and…"

And a sister to take care of. *Damn.* Once again, Adam felt like a heel. He'd been given the opportunity to follow every dream he'd even thought of having, while Callie had given up everything she'd ever wanted to do to provide for Gretchen. Talk about selfless.

Maybe he could balance the scale a little. For the next two, or four, or however many years this marriage lasted, he'd give Callie a shot at a few of her dreams. It was the least she deserved for putting up with him all this time.

And if, by some miracle, his body happened to be

one of those things she wanted, well, that was fine by him.

As long as she understood his heart was off-limits.

Chapter Ten

"If you could do anything, what would it be?"

With effort, Callie dragged her gaze away from the exquisite appetizer plate of fried zucchini blossoms and calamari. Adam sat across the restaurant's round table from her, making a basic blue shirt and khakis look far too good, his long, relaxed body in direct opposition to his laser-like gaze.

He sincerely wanted to know. But she wasn't sure she wanted to tell him.

"Wow." She blew out a breath. "That's kind of a loaded question when it comes from your boss."

Chuckling, he raised his water glass and took a long sip. His Adam's apple bobbed as he swallowed, and a twinge of jealousy nagged her at the fluidity of his movements. Regardless of what he was doing, he moved smoothly and with purpose. It was more than his physical agility, although she envied him in that department, too. He was something she wasn't, especially since their marriage—comfortable in his own skin.

And holy crap! How she longed to touch that skin. The very thought had her gulping her own ice water.

"You laugh," she said, after setting down her glass. "But it's a hard question to answer." She tossed her hair over her shoulder and shot him a haughty look. "I'm a girl with so many interests."

He grinned, then scooped a piece of calamari onto a plate that was so miniscule, Barbie and Ken would feel right at home. The restaurant was Adam's choice. It wasn't Calhoun's, but another five-star DC headliner she'd always wanted to try.

Boy, had she miscalculated the restaurant's glamour factor. Several notches up from "fancy," it blew her out of her comfort zone. At least her vintage black pantsuit held its own. All the tables were filled with women in their LBDs, eating off the same teeny white dishes. It appeared the more expensive the food, the less of it they served.

"You are," he agreed, after finishing a bite. "What's more, I have no doubt you can make a success of anything you pursue. But, if you had to pick one thing to really go after, what would it be?"

She bit her lip. This conversation was making her uneasy. Up until now, her life had never allowed for wishes or regrets, if that was what he was asking. She cut to the chase. "Are you firing me?"

He choked on a blossom, raising the unusually large cloth napkin to his mouth while he coughed. Small plates, huge napkins. She'd have to remember that if she ever hosted a dinner party.

"God, no," he said, when he'd recovered. "As far as I'm concerned, you're hired for life. But there must be something you've always dreamed of doing. For example, as a kid, I always wanted to write spy stories, couldn't get enough of them. I was reading Le Carré when I was eight."

"Impressive." *Note to self: Google that later to find out what the hell he's talking about.*

"I'd dream up these elaborate plots, most of which were too fantastic to ever see the light of day. But, after Mallory died, I was so stuck in my head and I needed a distraction so badly, I just sat down at the computer and went for it. Wolfe Bridges sprang, fully formed, onto the page."

"And the rest, as they say, is history." She smiled.

He returned it and added a nod. "That's another thing I've always had a passion for, history. I do what I love, Cal. I'm just wondering if you do too."

Okay. At least she wasn't about to lose her job. However, that didn't mean she was ready to blurt out any of the few youthful ambitions she'd held. "I do. I love working for you. It's interesting and challenging, and I love being on campus. All of it, helping you, helping the students. It's all good."

She thought it was a decent dodge, but Adam was a dog with a bone.

"Today, in the car, Gretchen said you'd studied art. Is that interest in the rearview mirror, or is it something you'd still like to pursue?"

Choosing what she hoped was the correct fork from the gleaming arsenal beside her plate, Callie speared a piece of calamari and set it on her itty-bitty plate. She toyed with it for a minute, knowing his gaze hadn't wavered.

She might as well quit stalling, because he'd wait until he got an answer he was satisfied with. "All right. I'll tell you. But you have to promise not to laugh."

He arched a brow. "You have to ask?"

No, she didn't. If she told anyone, it would be him and he would be incredibly supportive, because that was who he was. "I've always wanted to be a potter. I love working with clay."

He sat back in his chair, one elbow perched on the chair's low back, the picture of casual elegance. No wonder the hostess had taken such a long look when she'd seated them. Callie had used remarkable restraint not to shout, "Back off, bitch, he's mine!"

Because he wasn't. At best, she'd just borrowed him for a while, like a library book that would eventually be returned to all the gorgeous female books waiting on the shelves. Like Angela. Like Mallory, whose photos still filled the apartment they shared.

"That fits. You're creating something new, something better, out of the clay. It's the ultimate up-cycle."

Callie laughed. "I've never thought of it that way, but you're right. You start with this chunk of earth, and you can turn it into anything. It's incredible."

He grinned, in that adorable lopsided way, and his eyes glinted like a kid at his own birthday party. "There's a wheel and kiln at Mum's home studio. Every now and then, she has a potter guesting on the show, but for the most part, it just sits there, unused. She'd be happy to have you put it to good use."

A wave of longing welled up and lodged in her throat so stubbornly, it took two attempts to clear it. To work with clay again…wow. The idea was both enticing and terrifying.

"I don't know how good it would be. I mean, I haven't touched clay in years." Not since the accident, when she'd traded junior college for surgeries and rehab.

She popped the calamari into her mouth and an explosion of fried goodness, bathed in spicy marinara, hit her taste buds. "Oh. My. God," she said, around the bite. "This is amazing."

Adam forked another piece, straight from the serving tray into his mouth. It figured he could break the rules like that. He was among his people. If she did that, here of all places, she'd just look unsophisticated and garner pitying looks.

There was nothing worse than being pitied.

"It's delicious. But you're changing the subject."

She made a face. "I was hoping you'd allow it?"

A quick shake of his head indicated he wasn't budging. "Why don't I drop you at the studio in the morning? You can spend the day reacquainting yourself with some clay while my brothers and I continue our treasure hunt."

She helped herself to a second blossom. "If I agree, can we talk about something else?"

He looked at her for a long moment, a hint of a smile hovering along the corners of his mouth. "Sure," he said, finally. "I know talking about yourself is your least favorite subject."

Not quite true, but she didn't correct him. "I want to know about your search today. I take it you didn't find anything?"

He offered up the last bite of the appetizer and she accepted with gusto. Whatever the restaurant lacked in portion size, they made up for in taste. "Yes and no."

She looked up so fast she almost gave herself whiplash. "Okay, so tell me already. What's the 'yes' part?"

His eyes crinkled at the corners. "Whoa. It's not that exciting. Remember, I'm a history geek. Most of what we found will be of no interest to anyone else."

The knowledge that they shared this passion was more delicious than the food in front of her. "I'll be just as excited, and you know it. I had my doubts, though. What's left of the old kitchen didn't look very promising."

"It's mainly a pile of bricks," he agreed. "And most of what we dug up was more bricks, along with the usual broken bits of china, cutlery, and some shards of wine bottles."

At this, Callie couldn't help but tease him a little. "So, we know your ancestors set a nice table and liked a nice glass of wine. That much hasn't changed."

This prompted another one of his adorable grins. "And they were carnivores. We found the bone pit, too."

She smiled. "That makes sense; they're usually near the kitchen. I always find it funny that they used to bury carcasses. I can't imagine having some chicken for dinner, then going out, digging a hole, and covering up the bones."

"Not much choice before refrigeration and modern garbage collection. On a farm this size, the family dog couldn't keep up." Candlelight accentuated the playful glint in his eyes.

"Right." There was more, she could tell. "But that's not the exciting part of what you found."

His grin became a full-blown chuckle and her heart thumped in response.

"Nope, it isn't. When Jeep wasn't off playing with Gretchen or flirting with Eloise, he checked out the old fireplace. Behind it, right where it would have met the wall, he found a loose stone. It would have been far enough from the heat to be a safe hiding place."

"And?" Callie drummed her fingers on the table. "Spill it, buddy!"

He reached down and lifted his computer bag on to his lap. *Ah-ha.* Light dawned. It was unlike him to bring work to dinner, one of his mother's major no-no's, but now she basked in the realization that he'd planned, all along, to show her what he'd found. They were partners in this crazy treasure hunt.

Partners. What a lovely word.

After a bit of rummaging around, Adam withdrew an old ledger, its scarred leather binding falling apart at the seams, and handed it across the table. Holding her breath, she cleared a spot for it—small plates had their advantages—and opened the ancient cover.

Old-fashioned handwriting, the ink faded to a yellowish-brown, recorded a list of ingredients. "It's a recipe book! That's unusual, isn't it? I mean, household accounts are one thing, but a cookbook is another."

"True. Written cookbooks weren't really a thing then. But what excites me most is the marginalia."

She turned the pages, paying close attention to the smaller handwriting along the margins. *"Rebs closer every day. Father fearful we will have to abandon the farm,"* she read out loud. Then, on the next page, *"Father in touch with Aunt…"* Squinting, Callie tipped the book closer to the floating candle in the middle of the table. "It looks like 'Liddy,' maybe? *She has invited us to Phila. I hate the very thought."*

Mouth ajar, Callie connected with Adam's gaze while a small family of butterflies set up house in her stomach. "This must have been written right around the same time as the…" Pausing, she glanced around at the very public restaurant.

He nodded, without the words. "I think one of the daughters of the house was collecting the cooks' recipes. But, as she sat there, watching the kitchen work, she also jotted down her thoughts."

She closed the book and ran a light hand over the

frail cover. "You could publish this, Adam. As is, with the marginalia. It's remarkable."

He reached across the table and gave her hand a quick squeeze. Touch was big in the Hughes family and, God help her, she wasn't complaining. Emboldened, she returned the pressure, but instead of satisfying her, it left her wanting more.

Much, much more.

"I knew you'd get it!" He withdrew his hand after another squeeze. "Finding *the* book would be incredible, but I'm almost as excited about this." He tapped a forefinger on the ledger's top corner. "I'm changing course with the Civil War book. I want to publish the family journals, including this. I'd suggested it to Grandpa a long time ago, but at the time, we were both too busy to make it happen. We have a chance to tell the story of a unionist, non-slaveholding family living in the midst of the Confederacy. It's too good to pass up."

Her heart skipped a beat over his use of the plural pronoun. "You want me to help?" In the past, he'd done all his own research and writing before presenting her with a finished manuscript to edit. It had earned her a warm shout-out in the acknowledgements, but nothing more.

He laughed, probably because she was looking at him like he'd grown two heads. She needed to work on that. Expressing her true self in front of him was becoming a thing. *Stoic.* It was safer in the long run. This marriage had a sell-by date, and time waited for no woman.

And yet... They *were* married. A dangerous idea skirted around a corner of her mind.

Not now, damn it! The man is speaking to you.

Nodding, she hoped she hadn't missed anything important.

"—counting on it. The next Wolfe book goes to print soon, so I'm crazy-busy getting it proofed. Plus, you know what my course load is this semester. Would you start going through the journals? It'll be a big project." He shot her another one of those infectious grins. "We Hughes have always been long-winded, especially in written form. You'll want to start with the first mention of anything to do with antebellum politics, which could go back several years, decades even. You'll get co-authorship, of course. A fifty-fifty split."

At this, her jaw dropped so hard she was surprised it didn't hit the table. So much for stoicism. She clapped a hand over her mouth while battling a high tide of emotions. What he was offering went beyond generous, beyond thrilling.

"So, what do you think?" He leaned back in his chair once more, the picture of calm, as if he hadn't just rocked the living hell out of her world.

"What do I think? Where do I begin? I'm stunned. And excited. And a hundred other adjectives I can't think of right now. I mean, Adam…I don't have a college degree or anything."

He raised his eyebrows. "What does that have to do with anything? I know lots of people with multiple degrees who don't have half of your knowledge or love for history."

She swallowed. Hard. "That may be the nicest thing anyone's ever said to me."

It might have been a trick of the light, but she'd swear that her ultra-cool husband squirmed, just a little.

"So, you'll do it?"

"Yes!" *Duh.* She was a lot of things, but stupid wasn't one of them. To co-author a book with *the* Dr. Adam Hughes would boost her résumé and her bank account in ways she'd never dreamed possible. It wouldn't be a world-wide bestseller, but it was bound to be an academic home run.

And if that wasn't enough, tomorrow she'd sink her fingers in some clay for the first time in years.

Adam had just handed her a hefty dose of security and a chance to pursue something she truly loved. All that and a vintage dining room table.

It was a whole hell of a lot more than she deserved.

****

Adam stretched his legs out on the couch, gazing out of the living room's floor to ceiling windows at the city lights. Damn, life was good. Really good. Hearing the passion as Callie had spoken about working in clay, seeing excitement in the green depths of her eyes when they spoke about the journal, knowing what he could make happen…

It brought him alive again.

That was a difficult truth to swallow. Despite the occasional jabs from his family, he'd fooled himself into believing he'd managed well in the years since Mallory's death. After all, he had two successful jobs, plus a great relationship with his family and a pleasant place to live.

In fact, he'd been going through the motions, operating with a major disconnect. Since his marriage to Callie, his world had expanded, and he enjoyed the wider view.

He wasn't being altruistic about the history book. There was a tale in those journals and the old ledger that needed to be written, and Callie was the perfect person to do so. However, he was ashamed to admit it wouldn't have occurred to him to share the project with her, despite her endless competency, before their marriage.

The moment the ink had dried on that license, a partnership was born. Co-writing a book on his family was a natural extension of that.

He shoved another pillow behind his back just as Callie entered the living room from the kitchen, two steaming mugs of pungent coffee in her hands.

"Here you go. 'Order up,' as we used to say back in my waitress years."

He accepted the mug she offered and gestured for her to sit. She sank down in the black leather sling chair adjacent to the sofa and took a long sip.

"Mmm." She blew on her own cup. "I need this to warm me up. It gets cold fast once the sun goes down."

He studied the chair she sat in for a long minute. Hard, cold, and uncomfortable, just like the rest of his furniture. Just like his life, until she'd reawakened him to the joy of connection.

"What?" She glanced down at her chest. "Did I spill?"

With superhuman effort, he refrained from checking out her cleavage. "No. I was just thinking how unpleasant the decor is in here. That chair you're in, for example. In all honesty, I've never liked it."

She tapped on one of the chrome arms. "It's...stylish."

Meeting her mischievous look, he grinned back. "Admit it. You hate it."

Frowning, she patted the chair's arm again. "Hate is a strong word. I don't mind modern furniture. I just think it works better—for me—when it's mixed with stuff that's already been lived in."

He took a long sip and swallowed. "Nicely put, but you don't have to be diplomatic on my account. I'm sold on redoing the place, Callie Hughes-style." Sliding his sock-covered feet to the floor, he made room on the couch. "Why don't you move over here? This is the one piece of furniture in this room that's made to be sat upon."

She bit her lip, then stood. "Okay."

Her posture tense, she sat one cushion over, elbows tucked close as if to minimize how much space she filled. He wondered what it would take to get her to relax.

Besides *that.*

He shifted in his seat and searched for any topic that would take his mind off *that.* "So, you were a waitress?"

"In a galaxy far, far away, yes."

If possible, her spine straightened even more. *Message received.* Her past haunted her and, since he'd grilled her hard at dinner, he let the subject drop.

"Do you want to have sex?"

For the first time in his life, Adam spewed coffee. On his shirt, on the couch, and all over the white rug. *Sweet Jesus.*

"I-I don't mean like, right here, right now. I mean…" Callie drew in a deep breath and glanced at him sideways before her eyes dashed back to her half-empty coffee mug, as if it held answers. "We've agreed to this marriage for at least two years, and that's a long time to go without…*it*." She shrugged. "I was just wondering if maybe we should add that to our contract. You know." Her gaze ventured to and fro again. "If you want to, I mean."

If he wanted to. Did he want to keep on eating?

Breathing? But if they turned that corner, there was no going back. "It would change things," he pointed out.

Her gaze returned her mug. "It would."

"And you're all right with that?"

She took another sip. "I am. If…if you are."

Her voice, though faint, rang sincere. However, he was afraid to trust it just yet.

"Just to confirm, you're suggesting we put sex on the table. Wait, let me rephrase that," he said, as XXX-rated images of them together on the new dining room table flashed through his mind. "You're saying we add a codicil, regarding the possibility of a sexual relationship, to our marriage agreement?"

Terrific. He'd gone from sounding like a teenaged virgin to sounding like a freaking attorney. What came next? The old television cop routine of "just the facts, ma'am"?

With a heavy sigh, she set her coffee down on the glass-topped side table and jackknifed to face him. He had to hand it to her. She had to know she'd shocked the living hell out of him, but she wasn't backing down.

"Yes. That's exactly what I'm saying." Both her voice and her gaze were steadier now, more confident. Maybe they were headed toward "just the facts."

Blood pounded hard in his ears. "When would this start and when would it end?" He was beyond curious to hear how she envisioned this working.

Because it might be different from how he saw things. Any mention of love and he would head for high ground.

"Whenever we both want it to. When we're ready. The same goes for ending it," she said.

The knuckles of her interlaced fingers were white,

but other than that, she was calm. Which was more than he could say for himself.

Fake it until you can make it. "Okay."

Her wide-eyed double-take was laughable. *Good.* He wasn't the only one pretending to be cool.

"Wait. Is that a 'yes'?" she asked.

"Yes. You're right. Two years is a long time. We already know we like each other, care for each other. Plus, we're married and sharing space. Sounds like a win-win," he added, trying not to sound too much like Egbert the Legal Nerd.

"Right." She shot off the couch, wiping her palms on her sweatshirt. "I guess that's settled then. I'll be heading to bed. Alone. To sleep. Until you...until it's in the contract and we're ready and stuff." She grabbed her coffee mug and headed for the kitchen.

Adam remained where he was, still holding his lukewarm mug, attempting to get his head around this change in their status quo.

It would be both juvenile and ridiculous to make a fist pump in the still, silent room.

But as his wife's footsteps faded down the hallway, he made one anyway. Then he made a beeline for his study and the contract. Now that sex was involved, their legal agreement was more important than ever before. Legalese was technical, devoid of emotion, comforting. He cared for Callie, but the only two "L" words he welcomed into their relationship were "like" and "lust."

Anything deeper was too painful to go through again.

Chapter Eleven

"It is a truth universally acknowledged," Callie said under her breath, with a silent apology to Jane Austen, "that it is far easier to get a man into your bed when he's in the same town."

In fairness to Adam, his business trip had been planned for months. He hadn't gotten the hell out of Dodge in response to her bombshell of a question last week. A question that had surprised her, too.

However, whether he'd walked or run to the airport, the result was the same. He was gone, and with every passing day, she kicked herself for opening her big fat mouth.

She'd always been prone to verbal diarrhea.

Despite all that, sex with Adam was a good addition to their agreement. She possessed a healthy libido, and she was certain Adam did as well. And, damn it! Her visceral reaction to the looks other women gave him told her she wouldn't accept his sleeping with someone else with a dismissive wave and a help-yourself smile.

She wanted him. Bad. Yes, he'd always exuded a boatload of animal magnetism. But now that he'd checked a great deal of his work persona at the door? *Ooh, Mama! Danger ahead.*

It wasn't just a surface kind of thing, though. His personality was just as enticing as his face and form. He was smart, kind, funny. And that was just the appetizer plate.

The bottom line was, they could continue along their current path or take the plunge into a sexual relationship.

Right or wrong, she'd always been one hell of a plunger.

Saturday's dinner had given her confidence to go for what she wanted. He'd placed her on equal footing. That said, she could have broached the subject with more panache. Instead, the words had tumbled out, raw.

At first, she'd worried Adam was going to have a heart attack, right then and there. When he'd finally said "yes," she thought maybe *she'd* have a heart attack, right then and there.

"Callie, come see what I made!"

Callie finished washing the clay off her hands and rejoined her sister and Eloise at the stainless-steel table eating up the bulk of the real estate in Minna's pottery studio. Even if their relationship fell apart tomorrow, she would be grateful to Adam for reintroducing her to clay. A bubble of pride expanded in her chest as she surveyed the set of freshly fired mugs she'd made a few days ago.

One leaned more than the Tower of Pisa, while the handle on another had fallen off during firing—but the other two might hold liquid, and her glazing was perfection itself. Eclipsing all that, however, was the joy she'd experienced throughout the process. From now on, wherever life took her, she would find the time and place for playing with clay.

"Wow." Callie exchanged an amused look with Eloise before sitting down next to her sister on the glaze-spattered wooden bench.

Art had never been Gretchen's thing, but for all that, she looked very proud of the blob of clay sitting before her. "Do you like my unicorn?"

Callie gave herself a mental head slap. *Duh.* What else would it be? She hoped the giant protrusion at one end was its horn. "Love it. Are you finished?"

Gretchen's tongue clung to her upper lip as she turned her head this way and that. "I think so. Should I make a baby unicorn, too?"

"It's your project, so that's up to you." Callie looked over at the wheel, where her first attempt at a bowl sat in all its lopsided glory. Although headed for destruction, it had been good practice.

"When are you having your baby?"

Callie shook her head, hard. "My what, now?"

When Gretchen failed to answer, Callie sent Eloise a questioning look, but the young woman shrugged. "Gretchen Marie, what are you talking about?"

Gretchen gave her unicorn a few pokes. "Geez. You and Adam got married, so now you'll have a baby. That's how it works." She made a colossal eye-roll and pinched her creation a few more times.

Across the table, Eloise burst out laughing. "Don't look at me," she said, raising her hands. "This is the first I've heard of it."

"Gretch, honey. Adam and I are *not* having a baby." For a thousand and five reasons, the first of which was that they'd never had sex.

Yet.

Disappointment welled in Gretchen's gray eyes. "Why not? Babies are fun."

Eloise snorted, and Callie pinned her with a hard glare before turning back to her sister.

"Look, babies are cute and everything, but they are also a lot of hard work. Adam and I…" She struggled for the right words. "We're too busy doing other things right now."

Not the best answer in the world, but it appeared to satisfy Gretchen. "Okay. But, when you do have a baby, you should name it Betty."

Callie swallowed. Her sister could name a whole army of unicorns after their mother, but that was where that name stopped.

It was time for her favorite dodge. "Let's clean up our mess and go get some ice cream."

"Ice cream! Ice cream! We all want ice cream," Gretchen chanted.

"Sounds good to me."

Callie's heart stuttered as Adam, very GQ-ish in a crisp black suit, stepped into the studio.

"Adam!" Gretchen started toward her brother-in-law, and Callie had just enough presence of mind to grab the back of her sister's shirt and point to the studio sink. "Hold it. Wash first. Hug second." Callie released Gretchen as Adam reached her side.

He lifted one of her hands. "Yours look clean," he said, tugging her to her feet and threading his fingers through hers.

Certain she was floating, she glanced at her shoes. *Phew. Still on the ground.* Running her gaze up the long length of him, she inhaled his fresh, piney scent. Did the man ever sweat? Had she seen that Wile E. Coyote tie before?

Swallowing the lump in her throat, she reined in her scattered thoughts. This was the first time she'd seen him since she'd put sex on the table.

Oh, Lord. What an image. Was he this hot and bothered, too?

Hard to say, no pun intended. His expression was

pleasant and his eyes gleamed, but that could be a trick of the fluorescent lighting. *No.* Unless her radar was completely busted from lack of use, he wasn't signaling any awkwardness.

That made one of them.

He rubbed his thumbs along the backs of her hands, and something began throbbing. *Yowza.* When she'd put sex out there—be it on the table, in the bedroom, or anywhere else—she'd assumed they'd work their way up to it. But, if that radar was working, she'd have to adjust her timetable.

Or not. Gretchen, her hands dripping water, converted their quiet interlude into an enthusiastic, damp, group hug.

"How was your trip?" Callie asked him over her sister's head. "You're back early, aren't you?"

"A little." He grinned. "I missed you."

His eyes morphed into that glorious, stormy sea color, with a hungry edge.

Holy shit. He was looking at her the way the Big Bad Wolf must have looked at Grandma.

She had zero experience with flirtation. Make that less than zero. Into the minuses. Both of her exes had been decent but unromantic men of few words. Sweet, subtle, and sexy hadn't factored into her past relationships. So, what did she do now? Take a page from Angela's playbook and bat her eyelashes? Or worse, try to say something clever?

As if.

"I missed you too." Oh, God. That was anything but original.

Then Adam smiled and his eyes told her that, for once in her life, she'd said exactly the right thing.

****

Adam loved his sister-in-law. Honestly, he did. True, he hadn't known her all that long, but Gretchen had a way of brightening the world around her. As a bonus, her caregiver, Eloise, was also good company. Even Jeep seemed to like her, which was next to incredible, given his brother's single-minded focus on his naval career. But right now, Adam couldn't wait to get rid of them both.

He was at the end of a tiring, long week. The symposium he'd attended was prestigious, attracting some of the best thinkers in academia, and it was an honor just to rate an invite, let alone be asked to present. He'd needed his "A" game and, for the most part, he'd brought it. But it had required monumental effort.

Right now, he longed for time alone with his wife. Talking with her, laughing with her, letting that sexual chemistry simmer until they both craved the next step. Instead, he sat in a busy diner in one of the DC suburbs, his knees jammed against a Formica counter that predated his birth by at least fifty years.

Opposite Day. The antithesis of the evening he'd plotted all week.

He'd known from touching base with his mother that Callie would be at the studio, information that had made for some rather inventive thinking about how they might, in future, put a pottery wheel to good use.

His plan was sedate. Nothing flamboyant or over-thought. Something along the lines of whisking her away to their apartment, spending the evening talking over a home-cooked meal, and then letting time, their lips, and their fingers work their magic.

The not-over-thinking part was crucial, and hard to

combat since that was his usual MO. By some amazing twist of fate, he wasn't freaked out by this deepening relationship, but that could come to a screeching halt if he allowed the "what if's" to rule the day. It didn't matter how long it had taken them to get to this point or how bizarre their situation. They were adults who'd written their own rules, confident in what was off-limits and what was on.

Provided they ever got any alone time.

As if to confirm how far he was from reaching that goal, their waitress, a gruff platinum blonde of about fifty, sauntered up to the counter, her polyester uniform straight out of the 1960s, large earrings swinging so hard he was amazed she didn't hurt herself.

"Can I get you anything else?" She blew, then popped a bubble from the wad of gum filling her mouth.

He raised a questioning eyebrow to the group, acting, he hoped, as if he didn't mind if they stayed all night.

"I'm full." Gretchen giggled as she burped.

Thank God. Adam unlocked his phone and brought up the car service app, his thumb at the ready. *Boo-yah.* One silver SUV was right around the corner. Progress at last.

"Is this yours, handsome?" The waitress offered him the bill.

Nodding, he traded his phone for his wallet and paid, adding a generous tip.

"Hey," the waitress said, staring up at him as he handed her the cash. "Don't I know you?"

Seriously, this was happening now? When they were almost out the door?

"I don't think so," he said, inching toward the exit.

"Yeah, sure I do!" The waitress shook a finger at him. "You write the Wolfe Bridges books. I love those!" She pulled her own phone out of one of her apron pockets. "Do you mind?" she asked, holding it aloft for a selfie.

He looked over at Callie. She'd bent over to pick up the jacket Gretchen had dropped, giving him an eyeful of her rounded derriere.

Oh, he minded. Dear God, how he minded.

However, his momma hadn't raised any assholes, so he leaned in and played nice while the waitress chatted and took her photos. Then he jetted, sprinting into the parking lot and around the back end of an ancient Cadillac that was depositing several passengers at the diner's door.

He jogged up to the curb as their driver pulled to a stop and began ushering Callie, Gretchen, and Eloise into the vehicle's third row seat. No shot at intimate, whispered conversation on the ride home, then.

With a sigh, he climbed in beside the driver. This was turning into a very long night—and not in the way he had hoped.

As they merged into the traffic, his phone vibrated. *Mason.* They were a good twenty minutes away from dropping Gretchen, so he might as well answer it. "Hey."

"Hey. You back in town yet?"

Mason's voice, low and urgent, rang alarm bells. Adam leaned forward in his seat, like a pointer on the hunt. It took a lot to rattle his little brother. "What's wrong?"

"It's Mum. She's in the hospital."

Adam gripped the phone so hard his fingers stung. "What happened?"

"Crazy as it sounds, it looks like someone attacked her with a rock. Dad found her lying on the driveway, with her head..." Mason faltered, drawing in a deep breath before continuing. "Anyway, they're assessing her now."

"How bad is it?" Adam squeezed the words past the steel band of emotion constricting his throat.

"It's hard to say with a head wound. Dad says she's lost a lot of blood, but that's not unusual. She was conscious when I saw her, and that's always a good sign."

"Okay. I'm on my way. I assume she's at Washington General?"

"Yeah, in the ER. Dad argued for St. Anne's, since it's closer, but Mum insisted on coming to General because I'm here."

Adam managed a strangled laugh. "That's good news. If she was bossing people around in the ambulance, it can't be too bad."

Mason chuckled. "That's what I told Dad. I've got to call Jeep now. See you when you get here."

Adam ended the call and gave the driver their new destination before turning to face the trio of women two rows back. "We're going to have to make a quick detour, I'm afraid."

Across the SUV's empty second row of seats, his gaze collided with Callie's. Without a word, she released her seat belt and slid into the vacant seat behind him.

She fastened her new seat belt before leaning forward. "What is it?" she asked.

Matching her low volume, he relayed what his brother had said. "There's no need to worry Gretchen. I'll hop out at the hospital, and you can go on to her place, then head on home."

Callie looked at him for a long minute. Her green eyes reflected concern as well as something else. "Okay, if that's what you want."

Shit. It wasn't. That something else in her fleeting look? Resignation. She wanted to come too but wouldn't ask. It was becoming clear to him that she'd been left out of a lot of things in life.

He laced his fingers between hers. "Forgive me. I've been flying solo a long time. Of course, you're welcome to join me if you want to. In fact, I'd like you to."

She nodded emphatically. "Then I'm going." Glancing down at their joined hands, she squeezed slightly. "I don't understand. Why would someone attack your mother? She's the nicest woman on the planet."

"Well, you've never seen her mad." The attempt at levity did little to ease his nerves. "You're right, though. She doesn't have any enemies."

"Do you think this has anything to do with the German Bible?" she whispered.

"That's the first thought I had," he whispered back. "If so, this is getting scary. I don't know who this guy is, but he's obviously not afraid to get physical."

She nodded again. "Sounds kind of desperate, doesn't it? Or maybe he just likes hurting people, I don't know. Seems to me that there are better, more tactful ways to search."

"I think the guy's an amateur, acting for someone else." He shrugged his shoulders at the unspoken question on her face. "I have no idea who. But it makes me wonder if we couldn't set a trap for this guy, somehow."

She placed her free hand on top of their joined ones.

"Adam, I know you're upset about your mom. But remember, the police, FBI, and Secret Service are working on this. Let's leave any traps to them."

He sighed. "Yeah, you're right. I just hate the inaction."

It was his turn to give her fingers a reassuring squeeze. Her hands were smaller than his, her nails short, but well-groomed. Capable hands, like Callie herself. He ran his other hand over the back of hers, feeling her corresponding shiver.

Their eyes locked again and this time, he had no trouble reading her emotion.

Desire. Pure, simple, naked desire.

"Callie…"

She swallowed, the tip of her tongue flashing as she wet her lips.

"Yes?" Her breath, feather-light, teased his cheek.

He measured his words carefully, so as not to spook her. "I want you to know, this isn't what I had in mind for this evening."

Her eyes widened, and her mouth formed a little "o." She looked like she might speak, but before she could, he placed a finger to her lips. Straining against the seat belt, he leaned in and kissed her.

In the back, Gretchen giggled. "Ooh! Yuck."

Adam drew back with a rueful grin, the minty taste of Callie's lip balm on his tongue. This wasn't the time or the place, but she'd gotten his message.

Soon.

Chapter Twelve

Callie stood with her back to the huge stone hearth in the Hughes' sprawling, high-ceilinged family room. It was her favorite room in the house, the air redolent with the scent of old books and long extinguished wood fires. Her sister-in-law, Priss, stood next to her, wearing a slight expression of awe that matched Callie's own emotions. Calling the scene before them "overwhelming" was an understatement. The Hughes family in crisis mode was overwhelming on steroids.

The situation was as different from Callie's past as night was from day. Unbidden, memories of when she'd broken her arm as a child swirled in her head. Her parents, like the functional alcoholics they were, had gotten her the help she'd needed and conjured up a reasonable amount of parental anxiety at the hospital. That charade had lasted as far as the parking lot.

By the time they reached home, her folks had already finished round three of the Blame Game and were prepared for round four, thanks to a stop at the conveniently located neighborhood liquor store. The rest of that night was only too clear in Callie's mind.

Her parents had retired to their bedroom—their favorite place to drink and fight—leaving Callie to one-handedly fix a few sloppy PB & J's for herself and Gretchen. Sleep seldom came when her parents were engaged in World War III, and a throbbing arm had only exacerbated her childhood insomnia.

Now, knee-deep in the Hughes version of familial love, she couldn't stop hungering for what she'd missed. She'd long ago stopped being angry with her parents, but her hostility toward the disease that stole her childhood? That would be with her forever.

"Eighteen is my lucky number." Like a queen on her throne, Minna sat on the chaise end of the cream-colored leather couch. Patrick, Adam, and Jeep danced in attendance. Mason was still at the hospital.

"Don't know what's so lucky about eighteen stitches." Jeep's usual brusqueness was belied by the gentle way he fluffed the down-filled pillows at his mother's back.

"It's lucky, dearest, because it isn't nineteen," his mother said, raising an exploratory hand to the large rectangle of gauze that was taped to a shaved section on top of her head.

It was all too familiar.

Patrick gave his wife's hand a loud kiss. "No touching."

She pouted. "But the tape pulls."

Adam sat next to her, a steaming mug of tea in his hands. "Here, drink up. You always say there's nothing better than a nice cuppa."

Minna tossed her husband and sons fond looks as tears welled in her blue eyes. "Nothing, except family," she said, with a watery sob. Catching sight of Callie and Priss, she waved them over.

"That includes you wallflowers, too." She gave Adam a gentle shoulder nudge. "Enough of all this testosterone. Darling, do make room."

Adam winked at Callie and exchanged his spot on the couch for one of the large leather wing chairs flanking the fireplace. "Her Majesty awaits, ladies."

Priss, her pale face accentuating long, curly eyelashes Callie would kill for, moved first, sinking down onto the seat Adam had just vacated. "I'm so thankful you're going to be okay," she said, wrapping her arms around Minna.

"Thank you, my dear. As everyone here knows, I have a very hard head." Minna returned the hug with her usual enthusiasm, regardless of her injury.

Still shaken by old memories, Callie started across the room, her hip twinging from standing too long. As she passed Adam, he snaked an arm around her waist and drew her to his side, settling her onto the broad chair arm.

"I could use some support, too. It isn't every day one's mother is attacked," he said, keeping her within the circle of his arm.

Unlike the handholding he'd initiated earlier, this gesture wasn't flirty, just comforting, and Callie welcomed it far more than she should. No one enjoyed an evening at the hospital, but there were several reasons why they both hated it more than most.

"Yeah." Jeep collapsed in the twin chair on the other side of the hearth. "Speaking of, what the ficus is this all about?"

Callie couldn't help giving Jeep a thumbs-up in response to his unusually G-rated comment.

He gave a modest nod. "I'm giving Mum's ears a break, since she's been in the hospital."

Minna snorted. "Just for that, I'm charging you. Go put a check in the swear jar."

Jeep rolled his eyes and muttered something that sounded like "fucking scholarship" under his breath.

"What was that, dear?" Minna asked, sweetly.

"I said I'll Venmo you." Jeep folded his massive arms across the mile-wide expanse of his chest. "No one uses checks anymore."

Minna transferred her gaze to her husband, as if expecting him to either confirm or refute Jeep's statement, but Patrick, frowning hard, didn't respond. Instead, he left his spot on the chaise by his wife's feet and began to pace. His movements reminded Callie of Adam, the world's greatest pacer whenever he became worried.

"I don't like this. Any of it," Patrick declared, after a few passes.

"Let's see what the Feds have to say." Adam removed his arm from Callie's hips and pulled out his phone. "I sent an email to Agent Andrews earlier." Callie watched as he scrolled through his mailbox and opened a message.

"Andrews says she reached out to the sheriff's department but hasn't heard anything so far," he reported.

"That sounds about right." Patrick frowned. "I informed them of the similar attack on you, Callie, but they seem disinclined to connect the two."

"Figures." Jeep made a face. "Our little ol' county police don't want to get mixed up with the Feds if they can help it. But, if you ask me, the attack on you, Callie," he pointed a finger in her direction, "and this one on Mum, as well as the break-in at your place, are all related."

"Agreed," Adam said.

Callie scootched around for a better view of his face. His rumpled hair feathered across his furrowed brow, and tiny tension lines radiated like spiders' webs from the corners of his eyes.

"It can't be a coincidence that it all started with that magazine article and the mention of the Gutenberg." Adam glanced up at Callie. "Remind me to steer clear of magazine interviews from now on."

Patrick waved a hand. "It isn't your fault, Adam. I'm still not convinced of the whole Gutenberg angle. I'm willing to concede that a *Bible* might exist, but for all we know it might be whatever the equivalent of a Gideon was back then."

Callie chuckled at mention of the free copies of the Bible that had once been a staple of every hotel and motel room around the world.

Adam's own smile, however, faded fast. Shifting forward, he rested his elbows on his knees. "That's just what makes it possible that it *is* a Gutenberg, Dad. There wasn't any equivalent. If the family Bible dates back as far as it appears to, it must be a Gutenberg. But, as crazy as it sounds, what's even crazier is that someone *thinks* we've got a Gutenberg Bible hidden away somewhere. And they're willing to do whatever it takes to find it."

"I assume you don't remember anything leading up to getting bashed?" Jeep asked his mother.

Minna leaned down and straightened the folds of the hand-knitted throw covering her feet before tossing her eldest a pout. "I taught you never to assume anything, John. I remember it all quite well, thank you very much. I glanced out the living room window at just past six because Peter said he'd send a courier by with an updated copy of the script for Tuesday's taping." She turned to Priss. "I prefer the old, spiral-bound versions over an email file."

"Peter Gilbey is Mum's head writer," Adam

explained.

"It was dark, of course, but those new lights your father installed make the lawn glow like a football field." She held up a hand at Patrick's indrawn breath. "No, darling. They're wonderful. They'll be most helpful when we have company and—"

"Mum!" Adam and Jeep both barked out.

Minna's blue eyes widened. "Well, they will be. Now, where was I? Oh, yes. I saw a small, thin figure— a man, I think. He left the shadows of the outbuildings and crossed into the yard, heading toward the house." She lifted her ringed hands in a grand gesture. "Naturally, I assumed it was the courier, just a bit lost. I headed across the lawn to meet him, but he disappeared. In the next moment, I was coshed from behind."

Patrick stopped his pacing and frowned at his wife with a bucketload of disapproval. Any other situation and Callie would have been roaring with laughter.

"Of all the reckless... Min, you should have called me immediately."

"Then *you'd* have the stitches instead of me, and you're such a terrible patient, darling," Minna said, with the sort of airy logic Callie now recognized as her mother-in-law's trademark. "Besides, it wouldn't do to have the chief justice's head split open. Every judgment you'd hand down forever after would be cast into doubt. And just think of the paperwork."

Patrick looked as if he might say something, shook his head, and looked over at his sons in defeat. "I know better than to argue with her. In her own peculiar way, she's probably right."

"Did you just call me 'peculiar,' darling?"

Patrick leaned down and gave his wife a quick kiss

before returning to his seat by her side. "You know I did. What's more, I meant it."

Minna laughed and bracketed her husband's face with her hands. "Thank you. Life's infinitely more fun when you're peculiar."

Callie looked away, trying to swallow the Mount Everest-sized lump in her throat. It refused to budge. *This family*. Liking them this much just might be her undoing. Resisting Adam was difficult enough. Adding in his family threatened her heart, big time.

She took a couple deep breaths, in through her nose, out through her mouth. *No. Just no.* She would escape the vortex of love this family produced. It had always been Callie and Gretchen Against the World and it always would be. The tragedy of her past had made that much clear.

"Everything leads back to a small, thin man in dark clothing," she said, thinking out loud. "Of course, that could describe any number of men." She met Adam's eyes. "But it does seem like one heck of a coincidence."

His phone dinged, and he sat back, checking the screen. After scrolling for a moment, he looked over at Jeep. "Can you or one of your old SEAL buddies stay here tonight?"

Jeep nodded once. "One step ahead of you. My bag's in the car."

"Good."

A wave of uneasiness swept through Callie as she studied Adam's face. The set of his jaw, the pronounced worry lines. There was something he wasn't sharing.

"Of course, I always love having you, John, dear, but that's not necessary. I've promised your father I won't go wandering about alone again, and this house is safer than Buckingham Palace."

"That's a poor example, Minna my love. The palace has been broken into more than once," Patrick said, patting her knee.

She swatted her husband with an extra pillow. "You know what I mean."

"What aren't you telling us, Adam?" Jeep ordered before Callie could ask.

Adam's glance swept the room. "Bill Dobbs, our building's chief of security, went missing a few days ago."

"Missing?" The hairs on the back of Callie's neck tingled. "You didn't tell me that."

Adam slipped his arm around her waist again as he met her eyes. Reading their dark depths, she braced for bad news. Super bad news.

"There wasn't much to tell until now. They just found his body floating in the Potomac, riddled with bullet holes."

****

Adam sat back on the living room couch and closed his eyes. He was bone tired. They hadn't left his parents' house until they'd discussed Dobbs' murder six ways from Sunday and finalized plans for his parents' safety.

Jeep and his Navy friends were taking the lead but talk of armed patrols and more had made the already stressful night even more so. Now, the oversized, round, black-and-white clock over the mantel showed midnight and Adam's weary mind reeled from Agent Andrews' bombshell email. He couldn't think about anything else.

Well, *almost* anything else.

He sensed rather than heard Callie enter the room and opened his eyes. In her hands, she cradled a mug of steaming tea, and he found himself ridiculously glad to know she'd decided to stay up longer.

Mindful of her drink, she sat in her usual chair and settled in with her weight on her good hip, bare feet tucked under her. She'd changed into a pair of leggings and an oversized sweatshirt—an old one of his he'd loaned her a few days ago. Knowing something he'd once worn enfolded her curves hit him with an erotic force that was hard to ignore.

Rock hard.

With as much nonchalance as he could muster, he grabbed a throw pillow and dropped it in his lap. It wouldn't do for her to realize the mere sight of her these days was all it took to give him an uncontrollable boner.

This was new territory for him. Not the erection, of course, but this…uncertainty as to how to proceed. He'd surprised her by coming home early, and her shy pleasure in seeing him had rewarded him tenfold. But now, after the night they'd had, he didn't know where to start. Or if.

With a loud sigh, she set her mug on the glass-topped side table and lifted her knitting out of one of the many baskets now dotting the living room. The big, colorful pieces held everything from a fluffy, turquoise blue blanket—no doubt made by Callie—to a bunch of magazines.

Despite himself, he had to admit the room had never looked so warm and inviting. For the hundredth time, he reminded himself that all this cozy domesticity should be unsettling the hell out of him. He should, in the name of self-preservation, be thinking about that instead of focusing on taking their relationship to a more physical level, but it seemed that train, now covered by a throw pillow, had already left the station.

She dropped her knitting—something that was going to be bright orange—into her lap and covered a yawn with a hand.

"You don't need to stay up on my account."

Her eyes widened. "What? No." She hooked a stray strand of her unbound hair behind an ear. "I'm tired, but between the attack on your mom and Bill's murder, I can't settle. If I went to bed, I'd just lie there."

Yeah. He had a solution to *that* problem. He just wasn't sure how to suggest it.

"You're safe here. You know I won't let anything happen to you." Perfect. Now he sounded like a pompous, sexist ass. That was a sure way to get a woman into bed.

"What I mean is, we already know the security system works, and Agent Andrews said the DC police are stepping up patrols." *For the love of God, man, just shut up.*

She picked at the knitting in her lap. "No, it isn't that. I'm glad Jeep's staying with your parents, since their place is a little remote, but I feel safe here. It's all just so…so surreal, you know?" Picking up a loose end, she looped the yarn between her fingers, then let it fall. "I know we've been discussing it for hours, but I still find it difficult to take in." She shrugged, defensively. "I'm not being naive. I mean, I've lived in a questionable part of DC for five years. I know murders happen."

He smiled. "Wait. Did you just admit your apartment is in a shitty part of town?" Her continual defense of her apartment was such a bone of contention between them, he couldn't help himself.

Her pink lips curved, and those flirty dimples

flashed. "No. I said it was in a 'questionable' part of town. That's only halfway to shitty."

They both laughed, decreasing a bit of the evening's tension. But the release heightened his already sky-high libido. Anticipation sent a shiver through him. Time to finish this dance. They'd had a tough evening, and she was open to some companionship or she would have stayed in her room. Things didn't have to get hot and heavy, but they could afford to get a little warmer and weightier.

He patted the spot next to him on the couch. "Come here."

She glanced around the room, as if to make certain he was talking to her. The insecure action reminded him again of the magnitude of the step they were taking. That he hoped they were taking. Contract or not, a physical relationship upped the stakes of this marriage game they were playing. He would never hurt Callie on purpose, but sometimes situations became messy, despite the best of intentions.

However, maintaining their status quo for another two years or two weeks or even two days was no longer an option.

She dropped her knitting back into the basket and stood up, gripping the hem of her sweatshirt like a lifeline. A look at her eyes, unsure and questioning, prompted him to stand, too. Like everything else in this marriage, this would be a 50-50 partnership.

He would meet her halfway.

Chapter Thirteen

Wow.

Just...wow.

Callie lay motionless in Adam's arms, her naked back pressed against the hard contours of his abdomen, afraid to breathe.

Everything she'd ever known about sex before had been wrong.

It wasn't embarrassing, it wasn't quick, and it wasn't without orgasms. As in plural. Multiple. Many. Her husband's skilled fingers, lips, and tongue had played her body like a freaking Stradivarius during their nighttime adventures in wonderland.

And now, in the gray light of pre-dawn, she wanted him *again*.

This impulse to seduce was almost as eye-opening as the orgasms. In the past, self-consciousness about her scars and her uneven hips had made sex, even at its best, a tepid requirement of being in a relationship.

But one night with Adam had just changed all that. He hadn't insulted her body, he'd praised it, admired its resilience, embraced its imperfections. He hadn't dominated or demanded, he'd liberated and coaxed. Now, she craved the wild intensity of having him buried deep inside her, and she wasn't afraid to ask for it.

Not too afraid, anyway.

She'd nearly worked up the courage when he began to stir, in more ways than one.

"Mmmm." He buried his face in her hair and nuzzled her neck, sending delicious shivers down her spine. "Good morning."

Dear God. Just the sound of his voice, low and heavy with sleep, made her whimper. She wracked her brain for something clever to say.

But it appeared Adam wasn't in the mood for conversation. With a few wicked caresses, he had her primed and on her back. Not that she was complaining.

"You know, today is Saturday." She ran her hands up his firm chest, over his broad shoulders and down his back.

Even in the dim light, she saw the edges of his mouth quirk. He knew her well enough by now to know that, at least in her own mind, the verbal hairballs she often coughed up always made some kind of sense.

"And that's apropos to?"

She gave him a slow smile and damn near purred. "We can spend all day in bed."

He threw his head back and laughed with abandon, giving her a perfect view of the corded muscles in his neck. With a sense of wonder, she traced one with a fingertip, experiencing a tremendous surge of feminine power in reaction to his unrestrained response.

His laughter trailed off, but his face remained relaxed, perfect white teeth gleaming in the gray light as he stretched a hand to the open box of condoms on the bedside table.

"Do you have any ideas about how we can pass the time?" A nudge with his arousal gave her a big hint.

She caught her tongue between her teeth and inhaled as a wave of desire swept upward through her body, tightening her core and setting her nipples tingling.

"You know…" She snatched the foil packet from his fingers. "I just might."

****

Callie hummed into the shower's spray. This day just kept getting better and better.

First of all, they'd done IT four times in the past fourteen hours, a personal best by three, not that she was counting. Second, she'd never seen Adam this happy. Truly happy. Not the ingrained-good-manners kind of happy that ran only surface deep, but real, honest-to-goodness, enjoying-life-to-the-bone kind of happy. And third, he'd just run out for donuts. Did it get any better than this?

She couldn't imagine how.

They planned to eat way too much sugar and spend the rest of the day lounging around, cuddling, watching a few movies and—because she had all this newfound lust in her system and her husband was a man of exceptional stamina—making love.

Making *love*. In slow motion, Callie set the soap down and stepped into the full force of the shower's spray.

Oh, no.

No, no, no, no, no!

She couldn't be in love with Adam Hughes. That was a bad idea for about fifty-two reasons and a horrible idea for about twenty-three more. And yet…

It sure as hell felt like love.

As she stood there, rivulets of hot water coursing down her face, Gretchen's words came back to her. *Your eyes smile whenever you talk about him, silly.* Silly. That was all this was. An overreaction to the intimacy they'd shared.

Sure, Callie'd always had a thing for him. She'd have to be dead not to. He encouraged her to be her best self, which was no small feat considering all the baggage she carried from her childhood. But that wasn't love.

Affection, comfort, camaraderie, yes. Love, no.

Shit.

She lowered her forehead to the tiled wall of the shower. Who was she kidding? She was head over fucking heels for the absolute last person on earth she should have fallen for. To be honest, she'd been on that precipice for quite some time. Months, maybe even years. Maybe even from Day One.

So, what did it mean? She couldn't tell him. He'd made it clear he wasn't interested in love, in anything more than the friendly working relationship they'd always shared. In fact, sentences to that effect showed up at least twenty times in their marriage contract. Even the carefully worded addendum he'd written up regarding sex was couched in clinical terms. They were scratching an itch and nothing more.

Worse yet, he'd warned her. Sex changed things. She'd prepared for that in a hundred different ways, missing the one small detail that made the difference. She'd been half in love with him before they'd hopped into bed, and now she'd fallen all the way.

Damn it, she didn't *want* to be in love—with anyone. Love was dangerous and messy. According to her grandmother, her parents had once been madly in love with each other and look how well that turned out. In the end, all that obsession and jealousy just fueled their corrosive disease. So…

Nope. There was no way around it. The only person you could one-hundred percent depend upon in life was yourself. She'd learned that lesson at an early age and was proud of her self-reliance. She did what she needed to do to take care of herself and Gretchen.

Callie was resourceful, resilient, and independent. Love? Love dulled those skills. In fact, it was already happening. The relief and comfort she felt when Adam was at her side was addictive, and she came from addiction-prone stock.

But he was so damned hot. Kind, thoughtful, funny, intelligent. She'd turn into a prune standing there, naming all the things he was. She'd been unselfish her entire life. Right now, for one brief moment, she wanted something for herself.

The bathroom door opened, startling her out of her reverie. It had to be Adam. She wiped some fog away from the glass shower door and peered out.

There he stood, stark naked and fully aroused, two rainbow sprinkle frosted donuts in his hands.

"Delivery," he said, flashing a cocky grin.

Rational thought fled as she pushed open the shower door, unmindful of the overspray. He held the donuts high and dry while he kissed her, long, hard, and very, very thoroughly, imprinting himself on her lips and tongue.

Shit.

****

Friends with benefits.

Adam had doubted that type of relationship existed outside of the movies, but he was happy to discover he'd been dead wrong. It described their relationship perfectly. He and Callie were friends who also enjoyed one hell of a sex life together.

Of course, it helped that she was one hell of a

woman, both in bed and out. She'd kicked his sex drive up to Horny Teenager level and he wanted her at the oddest moments—at the breakfast table, when she was knitting, while they watched an Oscar-winning movie. Pretty much any time was "go" time for him these days. Wonder of wonders, it appeared to be mutual.

What a great problem to have.

But the greatest surprise—even more so than his super-powered libido—was just how much he enjoyed having Callie around. He couldn't remember the last time he'd spent an entire weekend with another person. Even his brothers didn't dare book more than an afternoon's worth of his time. For the first time, he understood that, ever since Mallory's death, he'd been balancing his social life with his "me" time, as if too much fun might be viewed as a betrayal of his late wife. That was absurd, of course, and Mal would have been the first to say so.

Now he understood what he'd been missing, all wrapped up in the tall, curvy woman who'd brought pleasure back into his life as well as his bed. And shower. And a few other places. When Callie left a room, the vibrancy disappeared. Little had he dreamed that this woman he'd known for years was the secret to bringing color to his monochrome world. She was damn near addictive.

That was the rub.

When he'd spoken to Mallory that last time, in that stark, sterile, *awful* emergency room, he'd promised he'd stay true. Her last request, as her life ebbed away, had been to "always remember." Through kisses and tears, he'd blubbered that he would.

However, in the past thirty-six fun, wonderful, lust-fueled hours, he hadn't remembered his late wife once.

Worse yet, he was beginning to think that maybe, just maybe, that was okay.

Guilt sucks.

He took a mug from the cupboard and jabbed at the brew button on the coffee maker. He always did his best thinking with a cup of coffee in his hand. Callie was in the shower, *again,* and tempting though it was, he was sitting this one out, giving his body and mind a rest. After one last, steamy spurt, the coffee machine finished. Grabbing the full mug, he sat down at the counter and tried to sort out his thoughts.

What he and Mallory had was once-in-a-lifetime. No one could ever take her place, and he'd spent six years avoiding any woman who dared try. He was beginning to realize and accept that he didn't need to actively conjure her memory throughout his day. She resided in his heart, and she wasn't just leasing the space, she *owned* a good chunk of it. Did that fulfill a deathbed promise? Maybe.

Damn it, why hedge? Mallory would always be with him, but that didn't mean he had to cut himself off from living. This acknowledgement, which had been pricking at his conscience for several weeks, brought with it a peace he'd never thought he'd experience again.

This brought him around to Callie, who, plain and simple, he enjoyed in every way possible. Not just the awesome sex. Her lack of demands. Her self-reliance. Selfish it might be, but he enjoyed the sense of freedom she gave him.

Mallory, sweetheart that she was, had been needy at times. Callie was anything but. She was her own woman, and he didn't have to make certain she was constantly entertained. In addition, she didn't have any ulterior motives or any messy emotions mucking up the works. He had that in writing.

Their marriage agreement spelled out the limitations of their relationship, both with and without sex, in clear terms. She'd signed on the dotted line knowing his heart wasn't up for grabs, and she was as honest as the day was long.

No, his emotions were in a tangle, not hers. Over the weekend—hell, who was he kidding? Over the past several *months,* he'd faced the realization he could be a living, emotive person again without ripping the bandage off his broken heart.

That was long overdue and immensely cathartic. But he had to make certain that this, *whatever* this was, with Callie, didn't become sticky. He liked her. A lot. They were good friends, on their way to becoming the best of friends and terrific partners at work. But love? No way. He'd been there and was never going back.

It had almost killed him when Mallory died. Call him a wimp, but he wasn't risking hurt like that again. He'd happily fallen into lust with his new wife, but that was where it stopped. He was still the boss of his own heart, damn it.

Scuffling noises snagged his attention and he rose to look down the hall. Callie, hind end first, dragged a fluffy, hot pink blob along the floor.

"I'm almost afraid to ask." He folded his arms across his chest to keep himself from grabbing her.

She bent over farther and peeked at him under her arm, apparently unmindful of her upside-down view. Her wet hair was corralled into its usual messy bun by one of those scrunchy things, and she wore what he now recognized as her pajama pants and a matching fleece top—items he'd promptly stripped off her when she'd slipped into them the night before.

"It's a bean bag. I had it stashed under my bed. I thought we might try it in the living room. It's super comfy. We don't have to keep it out there all the time. I know it doesn't exactly match the decor…" She stood and faced him, with a small shrug. "If you want to, that is."

Adam tilted his head and looked around her at the oversized cushion, imagining all kinds of uses for it that, judging by her uncertain expression, hadn't yet struck his wife. This could be fun.

"I don't know." He pursed his lips. "I think we'd better test drive it first."

"Oh, okay." She reached down to resume her towing.

With a laugh, he bypassed her and picked up the squishy bag. It was more awkward than heavy. He crossed the kitchen in a few strides and heaved the neon pinkness into the middle of the living room floor where it settled, listing slightly, like a giant hibiscus against the stark white carpet.

"Thanks." Callie followed him, slowing as she passed the kitchen counter. "Looks like you got our mail?"

Still fantasizing about their naked bodies sprawled across the bean bag, Adam grunted an affirmative.

"Huh."

He turned around at her puzzled sound. She had opened what looked like a bill and was staring at it, mouth open, confusion wrinkling her brow.

"Something wrong?"

"Um, no." She sounded unconvinced.

He started into the kitchen toward her, only to pull up short when she waved him off.

"No, it's nothing." Biting her lip, she refolded the paper into a neat rectangle and set it back on the counter. "I'll take care of it in a minute."

Stepping into the living room, she eyed the bright new addition, doubt written large across her face. "It's all wrong in here, I know. But everything else is so…"

"Uncomfortable?" Adam dropped into the fuzzy softness. Damn. It *was* comfy. Grabbing her hand, he tugged her onto his lap, ever mindful of her hip. "I like it."

Draping her arms around his neck, she laughed up at him. "Maybe we can tuck it into the elevator when we're not using it."

Laughter had her nipples brushing against his chest in an erotic way that revealed she wasn't wearing a bra under her shirt. The knowledge caused a swift reaction in his pants.

Callie quirked an eyebrow. "You're kidding!"

He bucked under her, nudging her bottom with all the subtlety of a sledgehammer. She had a way of making him want her so fast, he threw all finesse out the window. "I never kid about sex."

She bit her lip again and glanced down at the pink monstrosity. "I'm not sure I can—I mean, on the bag. I'm okay to sit on it, but my hip might not like…" Flushing, she left the rest of her words unsaid with a shrug.

Lifting her chin with a finger, he met her gaze. "Hey. Don't worry about it. That's why we have beds. In fact, we've tried your bed and my bed," he pointed out with a

185

grin, "but we haven't tried out the mattress in the back bedroom."

Relief swept her features and was highlighted by her dimples. "I'm up for it if you are."

He flexed his hips again. "Oh, I'm up for it, all right."

She rolled off his lap and onto her knees and, with the aid of a nearby chair arm, got to her feet. "Meet you there in five?"

His sprawled position afforded him a fabulous view of her butt. "Make it four."

With a small, gloating smile, she headed toward the bedrooms again. Adam chuckled as he stood. He hadn't been this randy in a long time. Maybe thirty-two was the new seventeen. At least for him.

He grabbed his now-cold coffee and walked to the sink. As he poured the brew down the drain, his gaze dropped to the bill Callie had left on the marble countertop. *$15,249.00.*

Shaking his head, he wondered how she planned to keep up with her sister's medical bills once their marriage ended. At least, he assumed this was for Gretchen. He scanned the top of the document.

Gretchen Wallis Culliver.

Culliver.

His stomach lurched as sirens blared in his head. Callie's last name was "Wallis," the name listed there as Gretchen's middle name. So, where did "Culliver," come into the picture? He had a good reason for wanting to know. A *really* good reason. Mallory had been killed by a drunk driver named John Culliver.

He set the empty mug down with a clank. All of a sudden, he wasn't horny anymore.

Chapter Fourteen

Callie removed the aqua throw pillows she'd added to the glaring whiteness of the guestroom bed, humming. She'd rather burst out singing, but her off-key voice might kill the mood. Adam wanted her. Again. If this kept up, there was no telling what might happen to her ego.

The sound of his steps reached her before he did, and she turned toward the door with a smile. Her man was in a mighty big hurry.

Without a word, he crossed the room in two giant strides and thrust a piece of paper into her chest. "You forgot this, *Ms. Culliver*."

Oh, God. She looked down at the crumpled bill while her stomach took a dive. He knew. After all these years, after all her careful dodges, *he knew*. "Adam, I can explain."

With a strangled laugh, he turned away from her, one hand pushing through his hair. "Oh, I think it's all quite clear. The one woman I trusted, with *everything*, is a filthy liar." He pivoted, and the savage look in his eyes stole her breath. "Just tell me this. Were you *ever* going to tell me that your father murdered my wife?"

Flinching, she took a step in his direction, but he held up both hands and backed away. She had to fix this and fast.

"I never intended to deceive you, but it was never the right moment. I intended to apologize that first day,

at my interview, but everything went so well, and…"
One hundred percent true, it sounded lame as hell, even to her, and she scoured her brain for better, more convincing words.

"I want you out. Today. Now."

The flatness of his voice was more decimating than his brutal gaze.

"No, Adam, please. We need to talk about this. If you'll just give me a chance to…"

With a sob, she realized the words she chose didn't matter. She was speaking to an empty room.

****

Callie wasn't much of a crier. For the most part, nothing short of a punch in the nose could make her weep. At least, that had been true five days ago.

Now, try as she might, she couldn't *stop* crying.

She pushed replay on the scene in Adam's back bedroom five hundred times a day, watching a constant loop of the stiff expanse of his back as he turned and left the room without a word.

She honestly, swear-on-her-grandmother's-grave, hadn't set out to deceive him. Well, not for this long. "Wallis" was her legal name and had been for years. She'd dropped the "Culliver" like a hot potato the minute she'd turned eighteen.

A few months before then, a brief and complete failure of a meeting with Mallory's parents had taught her she'd have no luck making amends for the accident under that name. So, the "Culliver" disappeared from the record, and Callie hadn't missed it.

The job with Adam had been a fluke. She'd kept tabs on him and Mallory's family ever since the accident, but she'd learned of his need for an assistant one day while checking the campus website for a now forgotten, unrelated reason.

She'd interviewed more for a chance to meet him and see for herself how he was doing than with the expectation she would land the position. However, life had thrown a curve ball when he offered her the job. It paid well and played to her strengths, something the waitressing gig she had at the time did not, and she'd grabbed at the opportunity.

For the most part, she'd never looked back. Until now.

She didn't blame Adam. All of this was her fault. Throughout the first couple of months that she'd worked for him, she'd looked for an opportunity to tell him about that fateful night, to explain how she'd pleaded with her father not to drive but had been powerless to stop him. How John Culliver had *run over his own daughter*, shattering Callie's hip and pelvis, before speeding off to cause the accident that had killed him, her mother, and Mallory Hughes. Thank God, Gretchen had been tucked away at their grandmother's house that weekend. That knowledge had been the only bright spot during those dark days.

However, as the weeks turned into months and then years, revealing her connection to Mallory's accident grew less and less vital. She'd told him everything but the explosive truth. They worked well together. He'd been pleased; she'd been pleased. It had been all too easy to convince herself to let the past stay in the past.

Now, all of that had changed. Closing her swollen eyes, she wiggled around, attempting to find a more comfortable position on the battered couch. After Adam had stormed off to his study that night, she'd tried several times to get him to speak with her again, but her pleas had met with stony silence. Except when he'd laughed in her face after she told him she'd tried making amends with Mallory's parents.

He was through with her. Dripping like a leaky faucet, Callie had packed a bag and left. Thankfully, the Thanksgiving break meant she could avoid the office, although she figured the chances of her still having a job were about nil.

Swallowing yet another lump of tears, she fidgeted again, knowing the comfort she craved wouldn't come from the couch or any other piece of furniture. Before, her tiny apartment, with its quirky colors and water-stained wall, had been a source of pride, an external statement of her resiliency and independence.

Now, it was depressing as hell. A reminder of all she had lost because of one giant omission in her biography. It wasn't Adam's fancy address she missed; it was the damn man himself. His kindness, his humor, his intelligence and, God help her, his touch.

Pulling a well-loved blanket up over her head, she snuggled into the one throw pillow she'd left behind when she'd moved. There was a reason she'd left it. It had all the comfort of a boulder, but maybe that was what she deserved.

Technically, today was Thanksgiving Day, but she wasn't in a holiday mood. Years ago, during an early snowstorm, Gretchen had gotten into the habit of spending the meal with her friends and neighbors at Great Oaks, so there was no reason for Callie to budge. Better to sleep through the day if possible, although rest had been avoiding her every bit as much as she'd been avoiding Adam.

Finally, exhaustion conquered her waking nightmares. She'd just fallen into the gray torpor between wakefulness and sleep when the banging began. Shrugging off a sense of déjà vu, she shoved the blanket aside and stood, despite the protests of her bad hip.

If her landlord pestered her one more time to come down and join him and his family for dinner, she might move to a hotel for the night. He was sweet, but what about "alone" didn't he understand?

"Pauly, I told you. I'm just not up to..." Her words dried up as she opened the door to reveal Adam, his eyes dull, his jaw tense.

"Get dressed."

His barked statement heightened her déjà vu and she wondered at the Groundhog Day moment. Was it all a dream? Could she go back and try it all again?

"My parents are expecting both of us for Thanksgiving, and that's what they're going to get."

Her lungs deflated. Nope. No do-overs for her. "I don't think..."

"No, of course not. Why should I expect you to think about how your actions might make other people feel?"

She winced but took it, knowing he had every right.

"I'm not fit company." Turning, she stepped away from the door, letting it swing shut behind her.

Glancing over a shoulder, she discovered he'd slipped inside and was leaning against the closed door, arms folded, impatience stamped across his face.

Crap on a cracker. He wasn't leaving without her.

Damn it. Truth was, she didn't want to hurt his family. It appeared she had no other choice.

Murmuring a curse that paid double into Minna's swear jar, Callie limped toward the old shutters in the corner that she'd fashioned into a dressing screen. Good golly. Three days of lying around watching Lifetime movies hadn't done her hip any favors. After a brief stretch, she stepped to the hanging bar that served as her closet and hauled out a gray pantsuit. In the dim light, it looked drab and lifeless.

Perfect. Instead of eating her feelings, she'd wear them. She peeked over the top of the screen. Adam, of course, was pristine in a crisp, blue, buttoned-down shirt and khakis. No cartoon tie, though, just boring old red and blue stripes.

Frowning, she re-examined her outfit, adding a thin, cranberry-colored turtleneck sweater and matching fringed scarf she'd knitted a few years back. There. That was as much holiday spirit as she could muster.

A whiff of Adam's scent hit her nose, triggering both a wave of longing and a spurt of anger. Why was he doing this? All of it? He should know her better by now. At the very least, he should hear her out.

She was ready to launch at him, have things out there and then, but he looked so sad, standing there, alone.

Good job, Cal. You really know how to destroy a guy.

He caught her look and jabbed a finger back and forth between them. "I haven't told my parents about any of this, and you won't either. We'll wait until the holiday is over. I don't want to ruin their Thanksgiving."

His voice was unemotional and firm.

Nailed it. He was in no mood to negotiate.

"I see." She shimmied out of the fleece joggers she'd been living in for the past several days and whipped the somewhat overripe sweatshirt over her head, moving as fast as she could.

Screen or no screen, hanging out wearing nothing but skin was not something she wanted to prolong. Not with Adam in the room. It brought back too many memories of what had been. But her doll-sized bathroom wasn't an option, unless she stood in the shower, so the screen was it.

"So, what?" She grabbed a stick of deodorant from the nearby dresser and applied it liberally, hoping it masked five days' worth of funk. "We act like everything is peachy-keen?"

That earned her The Look. "We act like adults, yes." He quirked an arrogant eyebrow. "Assuming you can handle that?"

She eyed the ceiling and counted to five, then added another five while she tugged on her pants. So, he was taking the cheap shots. *Breathe in, breathe out.* Things would only get worse if she got snippy.

"Fine by me," she said, through clenched teeth and the long neck of the sweater.

"Good."

"Feel free to go wait in the car. I promise I'll be there in a few." She tucked the sweater into her waistband before popping into the bathroom to lay siege to her hair. One look at that rat's nest told her that "a few" was optimistic.

"Yeah, right. In this neighborhood, you wouldn't even make it to the curb without getting mugged."

Callie paused in her search for a hairbrush and faced her reflection in the small, rectangular mirror, her shoulders slumping in defeat. Sarcasm. Always Adam's weapon of choice.

It was going to be a long afternoon.

****

Through the years, Adam had attended countless of his mother's dinner parties. They were legendary and with good reason. But Thanksgiving? That was her tour de force. Her *raison d'être*. Her jam.

Despite the stitches in her head, she'd done it again. The house looked and smelled magnificent. Any other Thanksgiving and the food, the family, the football, and the tryptophan would have him in a turkey-induced coma by five-thirty.

But this wasn't any other Thanksgiving. Today, with his beautiful, deceitful wife at his side, was the Thanksgiving from hell.

He'd prepared himself; had thought he could do it. Thought he was ready to see her, spend time with her after her blistering betrayal.

He'd been wrong.

Not because he hated her. He *wanted* to hate her. Wanted it with every fiber of his being. But, instead, he just…wanted. Wanted to go back to the way things had been before. To the way things had been when they'd been friends and lovers. Wanted her under him, against him, around him.

That really pissed him off.

He hadn't forgiven her, not by a long shot. But when she'd opened the door to her crappy apartment, looking like someone had shot her dog, all he'd wanted to do was take her in his arms.

What kind of a monster did that make him? Talk about a betrayal. He might as well go dance on Mallory's grave.

"The family's history gene skipped me, but I gotta admit, that's kinda cool. So where is it now? I'd love to see it," Mason said.

Adam turned as his little brother and Callie joined him on the screened-in porch that stretched along the back of the house. So much for grabbing a little alone time.

"We handed it over to the university's Rare Books Department. It's fragile, after being walled up in that chimney for so long. The librarian is making a copy, so the original doesn't get damaged." Callie's gaze met Adam's, before skittering off toward the old swing hanging at the far end of the porch.

"Gotcha. It's funny to think about something staying hidden for that long, isn't it?" Mason stepped next to Adam and breathed in the crisp outdoor air. "Ah, the smells of home. I had to get out of that kitchen before I ate the whole turkey by myself. I came straight from the hospital." As if on cue, his stomach gave a loud gurgle. He patted it with a laugh. "Missed my lunch again."

Out of the corner of his eye, Adam saw Callie shiver.

Mason jabbed him with an elbow. "Your wife looks cold. Aren't you going to be a gentleman and offer her your jacket?"

Adam buried his fists deeper into the pockets of his down-filled coat. "Callie knows how to take care of herself." Childish, yes, but he didn't give a damn.

"That's okay. I'm going to head back inside, see if your mother needs anything." After a long look Adam didn't bother to decipher, she walked back through the French door to the main house.

"Brrrrrrrr." Mason's voice dripped with sarcasm. "What the hell's going on between you two?"

Adam stared past the long expanse of yard to the

lazy ripples of the Potomac. He wasn't much of a sailor, but he wouldn't mind hopping on a boat right now, sailing away to any place but here.

"None of your business," he said succinctly.

For once, Mason let the subject drop. "Okay. I can take a hint. I just hope the make-up sex is worth it," he said over his shoulder, before he, too, re-entered the house.

Adam slid his hands out of his pockets and leaned on the ledge of the screen's wooden frame.

There would be no more sex with Callie, make-up or otherwise, which was fine. He didn't want to have sex with a woman who'd spent the past five years lying to him. In fact, he should be happy it was all but over.

But he wasn't. Because there also would be no laughter, no talks, and no connection, damn it.

At dinner, he sneaked a peek at Callie across the loaded dining room table. He had to hand it to her. She'd pulled it together, and he didn't think anyone, besides Mason, suspected anything was amiss. Currently, Jeep had her laughing so hard, she was dabbing at her eyes with her dinner napkin.

The pressure of a hand on his arm made him start.

"Adam, I do declare. You're as jumpy as a cat in a room full of rocking chairs." His mother's imitation of a Southern belle, mangled by her still-heavy British accent, had never failed to make him smile before today. Right now, though, the best he could manage was a weak grin.

"Sorry, Mum. I guess I'm a little distracted."

He lifted a large bowl of mashed potatoes, then set it down again as he spied the heaping helping already on his plate.

"A little?" She nodded down the table toward a gray-haired man with a snow-white Santa Claus beard. "Uncle Max could stand up and recite Longfellow bare-arsed and you wouldn't notice."

This time, Adam made it all the way to a smile. Max was a very big man.

"That would be hard to miss." Adam pushed some oyster stuffing around on his plate and earned another withering look from his mum.

"What is it?" she asked, reaching up to re-tape the bandage on her head. "Is it the Bible Hunt?"

His mother's use of Mason's name for their ongoing search triggered another watered-down grin.

"No. It's nothing." He cast another, furtive glance at Callie, then turned his attention back to his mother. "Did I ever tell you the last thing Mallory ever said to me?" It was a trick question; he'd never told a soul.

His mother's eyes widened. "No, dear. You didn't."

He took a deep breath. "She asked me to '*always remember.*'"

"Hmm," his mum said. "I wonder what she meant by that?"

Adam stared at her with some surprise. "What's there to wonder about? Obviously, she wanted me to always remember *her.*"

"Oh, no, darling. I don't think so." His mother's shiny bob swept her shoulders as she shook her head. "Mallory understood you well enough to know you would always carry a slight torch. In fact, that might have been her concern, that you'd pine away forever instead of letting yourself be happy again." She paused for a long minute. "Yes, I believe that's it. I think she was telling you to always remember to let yourself love. Much more in keeping with her personality—and yours, for that matter."

Adam's gaze fell to his plate again. *Always remember to let yourself love.* Was that what Mallory had been trying to tell him all those years ago? It did sound like something she might say. But if so, if she had meant that or something like it, what in the hell did he do with that information now?

Almost without conscious thought, he sought out Callie again, only to find she was no longer at the table. He caught Jeep's eyes and pointed at her empty seat.

"Back porch. Needed some air," Jeep shouted, cupping a hand around his mouth in an effort to be heard over the group.

Adam flashed a thumbs-up signal, then stowed his napkin beside his plate and stood. He could use some fresh air himself. "I'll be right back, Mum."

His mother, busy answering a question from one of their young neighbors, waved him away.

He headed straight to the bar in his father's study. He wasn't much of a drinker, and once he'd learned of her background, he practiced abstinence when Callie was around, but right now he needed a shot of something. His mother had given him a lot to think about.

He downed a fiery mouthful of his father's favorite bourbon and stepped out onto the adjoining porch. The temperature had dropped, and he rubbed his hands together as he glanced around.

No Callie.

Son of a bitch. If she'd called a car and snuck out...

But as soon as the idea occurred to him, he discarded it for two reasons. One, she would never leave without thanking his mother, and two, her cellphone and the fringy scarf she'd been wearing were lying on the stone floor.

A prickle of panic jabbed him as he picked up the phone. The screen was busted, the glass shattered into a useless spider web.

The prickle swelled, lodging in his throat as he left the porch for the yard.

"Callie!" He shouted her name several times, adrenaline surging through his veins.

Where was she? The lawn was empty, shifting his fear up another gear. Jeep had asked a buddy to keep an eye on the place while the guests were there, and the alarm was off. The guy, whom Jeep had called Levi, should be in plain sight, patrolling. Adam had seen him arrive earlier, after Mason and Callie had left him alone on the porch.

Acting more on instinct than reason, he ran back into the house. He hated to upset their holiday, but he needed his brothers' help right now.

Mustering a smile for the crowd, he set his hands on Jeep's broad shoulders and leaned down to whisper in his ear. "I want you to keep it cool, but I just found Callie's scarf and her broken phone lying on the porch floor, and I can't find her anywhere. Plus, your buddy is MIA in the yard. Can you help me search?"

Jeep barked out a laugh. "Man, I'd forgotten about that. Okay. I'll be right there."

He shot Adam a meaningful look and stood. Adam had a similar, whispered conversation with Mason, who quickly followed suit.

"Hey, Mum. Remember when we were kids and used to go out and run around the house to make room for more food?" Jeep gave Adam a playful shove. "Well, this guy just bet me good money I couldn't do it anymore."

"Me too," Mason chimed in, patting his stomach.

"Heaven forbid you lose a bet," Minna said, rolling her eyes. "It'll serve all three of you right if you make yourselves sick."

Adam started for the door with his brothers in tow, only to be blocked by his father. His old man could still move fast when he wanted to.

"Everything all right?" His dad's voice was low.

"I can't find Callie or Levi."

His father swore under his breath.

"It's probably nothing, Dad, but given everything that's been going on, the three of us are going to look around."

His father tilted his head toward the kitchen. "Do you want Peretti and Dottinger to help?"

Given his frantic frame of mind, Adam had been tempted to involve his grandfather's Secret Service detail but, in case this was a misunderstanding, he'd pressed pause.

Jeep spoke up. "I'll tell them what's going on, but their duty is to stay with Gramps. We'll call for reinforcements if necessary."

Patrick laid a hand on Adam's shoulder. "Okay. Keep me posted."

Adam nodded as he and his brothers left the room.

Once they reached the kitchen, where the agents were enjoying a small Thanksgiving of their own, Adam explained the situation one more time while he and his brothers donned their heavy jackets.

"I may be making a mountain out of a molehill," he admitted, zipping up his jacket. "Callie and I had a big argument the other day, so it's possible she just called a car and left, without realizing she'd dropped her phone."

"But you don't think so," Jeep said.

"But I don't think so." The truth of the words amped up Adam's already pounding heart.

"I'm sure we'll find them both in time for pumpkin pie." Mason donned a pair of gloves. He was using his Reassuring Doctor tone, which only freaked Adam out even more.

"Our guys performed the usual sweep of the area about an hour prior to our arrival with the President." Peretti, a top-notch agent who'd been assigned to his grandfather's detail for years, told Adam. "Everything looked good. No one here who shouldn't be here. However, we'll set the alarm and take another look around inside, just to be sure." The agent gestured toward the door. "Let us know, pronto, if you find something amiss out there. We can have half the agency over here in ten minutes, max, if we use the choppers."

"I will. Thanks," Adam said, and followed his brothers out the back door. Nice to know he had the force of a federal agency behind him, should he need it. He didn't take it for granted.

They'd only gone about twenty feet from the house when Jeep, always prepared, withdrew a small pair of binoculars from his coat pocket and trained them on the grassy expanse stretching out behind the house. "Levi should be in plain sight by now, walking the perimeter and keeping the house in view."

After making a couple of sweeps with the field glasses, he lowered them and met Adam's look. "I don't see him. And I don't like it."

The lump in Adam's throat grew to massive

proportions. Jeep wasn't one for hyperbole.

Mason wrapped an arm around Adam's shoulders and squeezed, but kept his eyes trained on Jeep. "Okay, Admiral. What do you need us to do?" he asked, totally cool and enviably calm.

Adam had never loved his brothers more.

Chapter Fifteen

"I swear, if you're after the Bible, I don't know where it is!" The sharp jab of the gun in her side reminded Callie who was running the show. It wasn't her.

"I told you to shut up."

The man's hand tightened like a vise around her upper arm. He was small but strong, and well-armed. He'd first gained her attention by holding a knife to her throat, but he'd switched to the gun when he frog-marched her away from the house, toward the outbuildings.

"Please." She looked sideways at him in the waning gray light, trying to memorize his features for later, if there *was* a later.

He was about her age, with dark hair and a nondescript face. Everything, from his brown eyes to his ordinary chin was completely unremarkable. He'd blend in anywhere.

Perfect. She'd been kidnapped by the Invisible Man.

"I mean it. I don't know a single, blessed thing." She couldn't say it enough.

He gave a tittering little laugh. "Sure, you don't. I've seen you poking around here with the rest of them. This way."

Yanking hard on her arm, he led her away from the main outbuildings and into a stand of trees so huge she guessed they pre-dated the United States. Her captor steered her deeper into the woods, over uneven, unfamiliar ground. While he appeared to know where he was going, she had no clue. As the trees choked out most of the already waning daylight, she stumbled several times, bare branches scratching her face and clawing at her hair.

"There." A shove sent her sprawling onto her knees. In the dim light, she could just see the glint of the gun, pointed right at her chest. "Open it up."

Shifting her weight off her bad hip, she glanced around at the underbrush. Open what up? Then she saw it, pitched like a roof, all but covered by dried leaves. A few swipes and she had uncovered a pair of old wooden cellar doors, their shiny new hinges and padlock in distinct contrast to the rusty but still solid hasp.

Ignoring the knife-like pain shooting down her leg, she struggled to her feet, brushing a hand along the prickly branches of a nearby bush. The strand of fluffy yarn she'd discovered in her pocket wasn't much of a breadcrumb, but maybe, by some miracle, it would work.

Then, before her captor got too interested in what she'd just done, she stepped forward again and heaved the doors open. A dark, gaping hole lay before her, earthen steps leading God knew where. She stumbled backward. Going down into that pit was a bad idea for about a hundred reasons, with "impossible to find" topping the list.

Panic clawed at her throat. Adam despised her. And he was busy at a family dinner. Chances were, he hadn't yet noticed she was gone and wouldn't care even if he had. No, that wasn't fair. He might be pissed, but he was decent to the core. If he figured out she was missing, he'd call out the National Guard, if necessary.

But that was a big "if." It could be ages before anyone realized she had been *abducted*, because that was, of course, completely bizarre, and so typically her kind of luck. When someone did figure it out, the chances of them searching for her *here* were slim to none.

So, she did what she did in good times and bad. Blurted out the first thing that came to her mind.

"Why are you kidnapping me?" She faced him. Tried but failed to keep her eyes on his instead of the gun, which wobbled, just a little bit, from side to side.

Was he nervous, or did he not know how to hold it? *Nervous.* She wasn't certain that was a positive thing. Usually the term "half-cocked" made her laugh, but she wasn't laughing now. Instead, the words just kept coming. "You know kidnapping's a federal crime, right? They'll put you in jail for a long, long time."

He stared back at her, eyes wide, as if wondering if she'd lost her mind. At this point, maybe she had.

Raising his free arm, he used the cuff of his dark sweatshirt to wipe his nose. "You need to shut the fuck up." He motioned toward the cellar entrance with the gun. "Move it."

Nope. Entering that dark pit was the last thing she wanted to do.

He braced the gun with both hands, aimed it at her heart, ready to make her go splat.

Okay, then. Down it is. But maybe she could stall. She began inching toward the black hole.

With a disgusted sound, he grabbed her arm again and dragged her to the steps. "Go."

"It's too dark down there. I can't see where I'm going." Okay, that was a B-plus attempt, at best.

Behind her came the metal click of the gun's cocking mechanism, and her stomach flipped in reaction. He was familiar enough with a gun to get that far. "Move it."

She moved.

The outside air was cold, but the temperature in the cellar was downright frigid, biting right through her suit and sweater. She'd picked a bad day to dress light. With his free hand, the man shut the doors behind himself, snuffing out the gray light that filtered down the rough stairway. He fumbled a moment, and she froze at the sound of a board being fitted into place.

He'd locked the door from the inside. *Wonderful.* This day just kept getting better.

"I'm not trying to be difficult, but I can't see a thing." Arguing with a man who held a gun wasn't super smart, but neither was tumbling to her death in a dark hole in the ground.

The man gave an audible sigh, as if she'd just asked for the moon, but turned on his cellphone flashlight. "There. Now, move."

The beam illuminated the five steps remaining and a portion of the cellar's dirt floor, its once-flat surface now gnarled with tree roots. Along the walls, rough-hewn log shelves, most in various states of decay, spoke of the cellar's original purpose.

She was in the old root cellar, a throwback to the days before electricity and modern grocery stores, when cool underground temperatures were a farmer's best bet for preserving vegetables throughout the long winter.

Did the family even know about this place? If they did, they'd never mentioned it. The Hughes family may have been farming this land for well over two hundred years, but they had given up the need for a root cellar several generations ago.

"Over there," the man said, clicking on a large, battery-powered lantern and directing its light into one corner.

An overturned crate and a sleeping bag indicated he'd been making himself at home in the dank, cobweb-filled dungeon. She shuffled into the space on leaden feet. Cozying together in his makeshift bedroom didn't have much appeal, but he wasn't offering a choice.

She tried another tack. "What if I agree to get the Bible for you? It's back at the house."

"Liar," the man snapped. "I heard you talking about it earlier. It's at the university. I figure maybe your husband and I will make a trade. I get the Bible; he gets you. *If* you behave yourself." He punctuated his statement with a little waggle of the gun.

Shit and double shit. He must have overheard their conversation on the porch earlier. Except, he'd missed one vital little detail: she and Mason had been discussing the recipe book, not the Bible. "That was a different book. The Bible is back at the house. I can get it for you."

The man hung the lantern from an iron ring in one of the ceiling beams and studied her for a long moment. "I don't believe you," he said finally.

She shrugged, hoping to look nonchalant, which was as far from the truth as flying pigs. "I can't help what you believe. But you could save yourself a lot of trouble if you'd just let me go get the Bible."

He inhaled deeply, as if trying to hang on to his nerves, and pointed a finger at the sleeping bag. "Sit." He remained about three feet away from where she sank down onto the bag's cold, slick exterior.

If this was a movie, she'd karate chop the gun out of his hand and save herself. But she was ninety-nine percent sure that wasn't a prop gun he was holding, and she was no movie star.

In the bluish light of the lantern, he looked tired and a little desperate, neither of which were particularly comforting. Desperate people did desperate things. Like shoot people.

"This is a fucking nightmare," he said.

She gulped at the irony. *He* thought it was a nightmare? The bastard should see it from her point of view.

"You have no idea who you're dealing with here." He waved the gun again. "Not me. I'm a fucking saint compared to my boss. Do you know what he did to that guy from your apartment building? Shot him full of holes, just because of the fuck-up with the alarm. Guy's a fucking psycho."

Ha! Takes one to know one.

As if he'd heard her thought, his eyes took on a wild look. "I have until tomorrow morning to get that Bible, so I'm gonna get it." He took a step closer. "And you're going to help me."

Sympathy, that was it. She'd sympathize with him. "Look, I understand. He sounds awful. But maybe, if you just turned yourself in—"

"Are you crazy? I'd be dead before I said one word. I'm telling you; this guy's connected." He leaned over her, bringing with him the stench of teeth that hadn't met a toothbrush in some time. "The only thing that'll save me is that Bible." He switched the gun to his other hand. "That's where you come in."

Without taking his eyes or the gun off her, he knelt

and felt around in the shadows before withdrawing a backpack. He started rummaging through it one-handed, then pulled out a coil of heavy nylon rope.

Callie scrambled backward until she hit the cold, dirt wall. "You don't have to do that. Just let me go. I promise, I won't tell anyone. I'll just get you the Bible, and everything will be okay."

He erupted into crazy laughter. *Oh, God.* This dude was definitely losing it. She swallowed as well as she could around the basketball-sized lump in her throat.

"Right. I just let you go, and all is forgiven, is that it? I don't think so." He set his gun on the floor but before she could react, he'd imprisoned both her wrists. In seconds, he had tied them together tightly. Then, he flexed another piece of rope. "Stretch out your feet, like a good girl."

"Yeah, I've never been good at doing what I'm told." She seized the moment, kicking like crazy, hoping to connect with his crotch, but willing to settle for any part of his body.

Then she stopped. There was something about having a gun held to your temple that made a person behave. Without so much as a breath, she submitted to being trussed up like Minna's Thanksgiving turkey.

"I don't want to hurt you," he said, tethering the rope that bound her wrists to another cast iron loop in the ceiling. "But I will if I have to." He gave one final tug on the knot, then stepped back to look over his handiwork.

"Okay." He withdrew his phone. "What's your husband's number?"

Callie practically sang the number, her spirits buoyed by the thought of any kind of contact with Adam. The sooner he understood she'd been kidnapped, the better.

The man tapped the number into his phone with one hand, keeping his gun in the other. "Good. I gotta go up toward the road to get cell coverage. You're gonna stay here and mind your manners, understand?"

He raised the phone. "Smile!" There was a blinding flash of light, then the sound of him heading up the stairs.

Violent shivers attacked her as the doors opened, then shut with a bang. The unmistakable snap of a padlock being shut echoed down the stairs.

She tugged at the ropes, but if anything, they tightened. All her life, she'd played the hand she'd been dealt without argument, and she'd held some pretty shitty cards in her time. But this outdistanced everything. Damn it, she'd never told Adam she loved him. Hadn't even hinted at it. He deserved to know, and she deserved to tell him. He might hate her for it, he might walk away, but love? Love was worth the chance.

She'd intended to spend her life avoiding deep connections, and she'd done just the opposite. Her roots ran deep, both with Gretchen and with Adam. How ironic that she'd finally discovered the value of love now, in this long-forgotten pit, waiting to be killed by a madman.

At least, for once in Callie's life, things couldn't get much worse.

Just then, the lantern clicked off, throwing the cellar into complete darkness.

****

Shit.

Despite the reassuring words of his brothers, Adam was coming apart at the seams. Any minute now, little pieces of him would litter the ground.

Where in the hell was she?

His gut gnawed at him. None of this was like Callie and he knew, as certainly as he knew his own name, she was in trouble.

"Hey." Mason put a heavy hand on his shoulder and gave him a gentle shake. "She hasn't been gone very long. We'll find her."

Adam nodded his agreement, but this was a big farm with lots of good hiding places. It would take hours to search them all.

Plus, there was a murderer out there. If he lost Callie…

Jeep rounded the corner of the house with a large duffel bag slung over one shoulder and held out a walkie-talkie. "Here. Take this."

Adam took it, staring down at the boxy device as numbness spread through his body. It felt heavy and surreal in his hand. He was a college professor, for Christ's sake. This was as alien to him as the surface of Mars. However, he'd do anything for Callie. Anything.

That truth struck him like a Mack truck, almost sending him to his knees. God, he'd been a complete ass.

Gulping back the wave of emotion, he put that revelation on hold. First, they had to find her. Then he could call himself every name in the book.

"There's no sign of Callie or Levi back here. Did you turn up anything in the front?" he asked.

"No." Jeep unzipped the duffel. If Adam's questions had fazed him, it didn't show, and Adam envied his calm. "The yard was clear to the perimeter and there are too many tire tracks on the gravel for that to be any help," Jeep said. His clipped, military manner was oddly comforting. No one was more capable in a tense situation than Adam's bad-ass, SEAL-trained brother.

"And by perimeter, you mean road?" Mason asked.

Jeep shot him a masterful look which more than answered the question. "There's no moon tonight, and I've only got two sets of these," he said, hauling out night goggles and handing one pair to Mason. "But we know the terrain better than anyone, so that's to our advantage." He handed Adam a high-powered flashlight and placed another by his own feet.

Mason whistled. "Jeez, Admiral. Leave it to you to carry frickin' combat gear around in your car."

Jeep grunted and took out a rifle without blinking an eye, as if it were something as mundane as a cellphone or a set of car keys. Adam tried not to hyperventilate as Jeep made sure it was ready for firing with a few practiced moves.

"First of all, I drive a truck, not a car." Jeep slipped the rifle strap over his shoulder and stood. "Second, I learned a long time ago you've got to be prepared for anything."

A shadow flitted across Jeep's stoic face, reminding Adam how little they knew about his older brother's time with the SEALs. More than once, Adam had suspected Jeep still fought a few demons from that time, but right now, his brother's psyche was the last thing he was worried about.

Jeep's phone dinged, and he checked the incoming text. "I'm packing light today, but I called for backup. Once Magpie, Scout, and Trigger get here, we can do a first-class job of figuring out what kind of situation we've got here. There's a lot of territory to cover and we need to do it as fast as possible. But that doesn't mean we get stupid."

"Do you know anybody without a nickname?" Mason asked. "Even Levi's real name is David. He said you guys call him Levi because they're his favorite jeans."

Jeep's teeth flashed in the waning light. "Navy 101. Breeds familiarity. Like a family, *Little Bro*."

"Point taken," Mason said, with an answering grin.

"Okay. I'll head up to the road and wait for my guys," Jeep said, back in charge. "In the meantime, you two check out the old boathouse. Maybe there's a chance Callie lost her mind and decided now was a good time to search for some more tables or something. Use the talkie to communicate. It's more reliable than our cells out here."

Adam nodded, swallowing with difficulty. "Thanks. I can't tell you…"

"Then don't," Jeep said, with another tight smile.

"Besides, we already know. Now, let's hit it." Mason gave Adam a gentle shove in the direction of the boathouse, and they headed off.

Memories resurfaced of the night Adam and Callie escaped the party and discovered the note that began the Bible Hunt. Right now, he would gladly trade a Gutenberg, or three, to find her inside, sifting through old junk.

But as they crested the hill and began their way down the stone path toward the river, his heart plummeted to his feet. The building was dark. He and Mason entered, flipped on all the lights, and searched it from bottom to top, just in case.

"Boathouse is empty," Adam told Jeep via the walkie-talkie.

"Copy that. Proceed to the new barn. We'll meet you

there. Over."

"Roger that," Adam answered, maxing out his walkie-talkie vernacular. "Let's go."

Mason followed him out and down the boathouse's creaky steps to the uphill path leading past the woods to the other outbuildings. "So, you want to tell me what's going on between you and Callie?"

Despite the darkness that surrounded them, Adam sent his brother The Look. "I told you I didn't want to talk about it."

"No. You told me it was none of my business, which it isn't. But I'm asking anyway. Given the situation and everything."

"I'm in love with her." The words burst forth, without Adam's permission, their truth shaking him to his core. *Amazing.*

Mason bobbled the flashlight, and the beam left the path and illuminated the woods for a moment. "I knew it!" he crowed. "That's terrific news!"

"Yeah, well. There's a small detail she forgot to mention that's made things a little difficult." Although right now, in the midst of this frantic race to find her safe and sound, it did seem small, or at least not quite as huge as it had been. "Turns out her father was the drunk driver who killed Mallory."

The flashlight wavered again as Mason exhaled. "Shit."

Adam caught the bucketload of emotion behind the word because his younger brother almost never swore.

"Poor kid," Mason said. "That must be rough on her."

The misplaced sympathy rankled. "Yeah, it's rough. Rough on *me*. I'm the one who lost his wife."

"Yeah, but Mallory wasn't the only victim. Callie lost her dad, *and* she has to live with the knowledge that his poor judgment took the life of an innocent woman."

Adam sighed. Leave it to Dr. Mason to sense everyone's wounds. "When you put it that way, I almost hate to tell you the rest."

"The rest?"

"Yeah. Her mother died in the accident, too. Callie was badly injured, although I'm not sure how. I was too angry to let her explain." Which, he understood now, was unfair. The least he could have done was listen to her explanation.

"I get why you're mad. It's a big shock," Mason admitted. "But, knowing Callie, I doubt she ever meant to hurt you. My guess is she was running a whole gamut of emotions. Then, later... I mean, it's not exactly something you just blurt out."

"Like I said, Doc, when you put it that way." Adam pulled off his woolen beanie and shoved a hand through his hat hair. "Right now, I don't know how I feel about any of it. I just know we need to find her. What would you say is the best hiding place on the farm?"

Mason glanced over at Adam. "C'mon, man. You know I was the king of hide-and-seek."

A distant memory of an epic game struck Adam. "The hayloft, over in the old horse barn?"

The hood of Mason's jacket rustled as he nodded. "Took you guys more than six hours to find me."

"I remember. Mum nearly killed us. But it's out of the way. The outbuildings are more obvious."

Mason shrugged. "That's just what makes it perfect. We know someone's been prowling around for a couple of weeks or more, and it's not like the barn's that hard to find. The old tractor path leads right to it."

Adam glanced in the direction of the old barn. Nearly a half mile away, it wasn't visible from the house due to the rolling hills. But Mason was right. An old, rutted path led straight to its doors.

Adam lifted the walkie-talkie with a shaking hand. "Jeep. We have an idea."

Chapter Sixteen

Life was weird. There she was, bound, trapped, surrounded on all sides by cold, damp darkness, and all she could think about was the feel of Adam's body against hers. Memories of the heat of him, his voice and touch, helped keep the wolves of panic at bay.

But, like any good wolves, they were sneaking up on her, sniffing here and there to discover if she was a worthy adversary, or if she might surrender to hysteria at any moment. Personally, her money was on surrender.

That was not the way she wanted this to go. Throughout good times and bad, she'd prided herself on never losing her cool, and to start now, in what might be the last few hours of her life, would make her the ultimate quitter.

So, gathering what was left of her flagging mental and physical strength, she attempted, for the eight-hundredth time, to free herself.

"Aaaargh!" She put every muscle into the effort. *Nothing.* She was well and truly stuck.

Or was she?

Closing her eyes, she summoned a memory of the iron hook in the ceiling. It wasn't a hook, so much as an eye—a closed loop from which hooks holding different foodstuffs had been suspended. It had to be screwed into the ceiling beam, right? The rope binding her wrists had been fed through it.

With awkward, seesaw-like movements, a little bit

of rolling, and a blinding amount of pain in her hip, she made it to her feet. Breathless and sore from the effort, she promised herself she would do more ab work if she survived.

After a few achy hops to ramp up her circulation, she began to turn in a counterclockwise direction. *Righty-tighty, lefty-loosey*, her grandmother had always said. If she was to achieve enough leverage to unscrew the iron loop from the ceiling beam, she would be lefty-loosening herself dizzy, but if this worked, it would be worth it.

Slowly, the ropes holding her grew taut, then twisted, biting into her wrists with even more pressure than before. An increase of resistance told her she had reached the metal loop. The million-dollar question now was, would it turn?

With her feet tied together and her arms up and over her head, it was difficult to get any traction, but she kept at it. A shower of something covered her face. *Oh, Lord. Please no creepy-crawlies.* She spat out the dirt and kept up the pressure. With a screech rivaling nails on a chalkboard, the loop gave a quarter of an inch.

Yesss!

It was a painstaking process. She'd take watching paint dry every time over this. Several times, aching muscles and numbness forced her to unwind long enough to allow some circulation to return to her hands before she started up again.

Her wrists grew warm and sticky as friction rubbed them raw, but she persevered. This was her only chance. She would free herself or die trying.

Adam. Even though the chasm between them rivaled the Grand Canyon, he'd look for her, find her. Then she'd do some hard-core apologizing. The misunderstanding between them was one hundred percent her fault.

Okay, ninety-nine percent hers, but she'd take all the blame anyway because she'd taken the easy way out. Instead of fighting for them, she'd crawled off to her apartment and wallowed in self-pity. Totally not her. Whether it saved her marriage or not, she'd fight to explain, give it everything she had.

If she didn't die in this damn hole first.

With a loud crack and another shower of dirt, the ancient wood gave out, sending Callie, the loop, and the rope crashing to the floor. *Victory.*

Pain reverberated in her hip, but she barely registered it. She coughed out another mouthful of dirt and brushed tears away with numb fingers.

This was no time to burst out bawling or rest on her laurels. The man might return at any moment. She had to find the damn steps.

Dragging the heavy loop behind her, she crawled in ever-widening circles until she bumped into a shelf. After a few more fumbles, her bearings returned, and she inched over to the steps, scooting up them on her backside until she bumped her head against the solid wooden doors.

Adrenaline took over as she repeatedly slammed her shoulder against them. Once, twice, three times, she threw her full weight against them, but to no avail.

They stubbornly refused to budge.

****

"I don't know how much longer I can stand this, Dad."

Patrick drew Adam in for a side hug. "I know, son.

But Jeep and his buddies found Levi. You'll find Callie next."

Adam was relieved his father refrained from adding "safe and sound." He'd heard the phrase a thousand times in the past half hour; it hadn't brought him any comfort the first time he'd heard it, and it wouldn't help now.

Mere feet away, a woozy Levi was stretched out on one of the revamped barn's fancy new sofas while Mason doctored his head and checked his vitals. Jeep stepped away from the nearby huddle of ex-military personnel, who'd found their buddy unconscious in a ditch.

"What's the update?" Adam asked his brother.

"He should be fine, but he has no idea what happened. That's not a surprise, considering he was hit over the head with half a tree. He was bound, gagged and tossed into the ditch that runs along the drive. Whoever did this meant for Levi to stay hidden. He was well-camouflaged with old branches and leaves, otherwise we would have spotted him sooner. Mace called the paramedics, and they should be here soon to take him to the hospital for tests. He has one hell of a headache, but for the most part he's just royally pissed off."

"I'm glad he's okay." It was the truth, but Adam worried over the delay. "Now, are we finally ready to find my wife?"

Jeep nodded and glanced down at his watch. "Yes. In just a few minutes. I'm waiting for the authorities to show up. Now that we've confirmed this isn't some giant misunderstanding, we need more back-up."

Adam started to protest but shut his mouth when his father raised a hand.

"I know it seems like it's taking forever, but Callie's only been missing about an hour. There's protocol to follow in these situations, and no one knows it better than your brother."

"Dad's right." Jeep's agreement was without ego. "Doing this right helps everyone. Callie, me, even your sorry ass. You've got to promise me you won't go all vigilante on me now."

Adam was about to inform Jeep of his point of view when his pocket began to vibrate, and he dug for his phone. He didn't recognize the number, but now wasn't the time to ignore a call. "Hello."

"Is this Adam Hughes?"

"Yes," he snapped, tempted to hang up.

The last thing he needed right now was some guy trying to sell him siding or a new roof, and on Thanksgiving of all days. Was there no shame?

"I have your wife."

Adam stiffened and pushed the speaker button.

"Where is she?"

"Keep your pants on. She's safe…for now. But you have something I want."

Both Jeep and his father leaned in, listening. Jeep waved his friends over with a quick jerk of his hand. One of them got busy tapping on a tablet.

"How much?" Adam swallowed, wondering how fast he could free up some major cash.

"The Gutenberg. And fifty grand. I'm giving you the discount rate since it's a holiday."

As the gaping pit in his stomach widened, Adam met Jeep's steady gaze. The money was easy compared with a rare book that might or might not exist.

Jeep nodded and waved his hand in a circle,

prompting Adam to stretch out the conversation.

"Okay." Adam hoped his brother had a plan because he sure as hell didn't. "Let me speak to Callie."

"Nope. No chitchat, but I have a little present for you." The man laughed, as if he'd said something hilarious.

Sadistic little prick. The phone vibrated again, and Adam clicked on the incoming file. A photo of Callie, bound and gagged, filled the small screen.

"You bastard!" The words escaped before Adam registered them. His anger was palpable, a living, breathing thing coiled inside him, ready to beat the living shit out of this unidentified man.

"Sure."

The agreeable sneer enraged Adam even more. "Where is she, you son of a—" He broke off as Jeep's vise-like grip clamped around his arm.

"For me to know and you to find out," the man said, in a sing-song voice.

"Okay." Adam gritted his teeth so hard they hurt. "Where do we make the trade?"

"You know the scenic overlook near your house?"

"The one a few miles away, toward the city?"

"That's the one. You drop the Bible and the money, in a backpack, under the cement bench nearest the river, at midnight tonight. Then you leave. Immediately. Once I've verified the contents, I'll tell you where you can find your wife. Bring in the cops or try to be a hero and the deal is off. Understand?"

Jeep nodded.

"Okay." Adam raised the phone closer to his mouth. "But know this, if you harm one hair on her head—"

The man hung up before he finished.

"Got it," the ex-SEAL with the tablet said. "Got everything, in fact."

Jeep flashed a smile. "No kidding?" He leaned over the tablet, then rubbed his hands together. "Would you look at that! We're dealing with an amateur, boys." The navy buddies smiled and began exchanging fist bumps.

"What are you talking about?" Adam clenched his own hands. If one more guy, including his brother, cracked another smile, he'd get a different kind of fist bump.

"He's not using a burner. We've got his name, address—hell, we've got his fucking social." Jeep flipped a thumb toward the tablet. "And we've pinpointed the area he's calling from."

Adam looked at the device. "You did all that from here? On that thing?"

The man with the tablet avoided Adam's gaze. "It, um, might not be strictly legal."

"Fuck legal. Let's go get the bastard! I want my wife back." Adam took a step toward the assortment of cars parked in the driveway, but both his father and brother held him back.

"Wait a minute, son. Let's hear the plan first."

Jeep handed the tablet back to his friend and gestured at Adam. "Let me see that photo of Callie."

Adam passed him his phone. "Go ahead. It makes me sick to look at it."

Jeep opened the photo, turned the phone sideways, zoomed in and out. "Son of a bitch," he said, smiling. He handed the phone back to Adam. "Recognize that?"

Gathering his strength, Adam glanced down at the image. Jeep had enlarged the photo until Callie was nothing but a fuzzy sliver of gray along the left side, zooming in on something on the right. What was it? Adam squinted hard.

"Is that…?" He held his breath and gave the phone to his dad. Nobody could navigate the grounds of the farm better than his old man.

"That's the old root cellar. Those log shelves are distinctive."

Jeep nodded. "And it's not far from where the call was made."

"We can be there in less than ten minutes. Let's go." Adam headed for the door.

Jeep set a hand on Adam's arm, then addressed his team. "We'll start the search the way we planned, starting with where that signal was and working backward. Magpie, call the locals, and fill them in," he instructed. "I'll send the coordinates when we get to the root cellar. Here, take the night goggles. We won't need them. We know the terrain."

All three of the navy men nodded as they accepted the gear. "We'll get the sumbitch. Easy," the man with the tablet said.

"Okay. Mason, I hear sirens. Are you with us?"

Mason patted his patient on the shoulder and stood. "Yep. The EMTs will know what to do." He glanced over at their father. "Everyone okay inside?"

"Fine. I had to sit on your mother to keep her from joining the search, but everyone's hanging in there. Peretti and Dottinger are with Grandpa. We're safe as houses." Adam's father's mouth twisted, as if he wanted to add something.

"No," Adam said, before his father could continue. "We need you here, directing the EMTs. Then I want you to go back to the house, arm the alarm, and wait for the police."

"I agree," Jeep said, firing up his own flashlight.

"Right." After a lingering look at his sons, Patrick sat down in a chair near Levi, waving his walkie-talkie. "I'll be listening."

"Okay. Now let's go." Adam was coming out of his skin.

Jeep sidestepped, beating Adam through the door to the yard. He patted the rifle that still hung on his shoulder. "We're doing this the right way, remember? You come *after* me since I'm the one with the weapon."

Adam glared at Jeep's back. He had no death wish, but if his brother thought he was going to cower behind him or some fucking bush somewhere, he could think again.

Jeep snorted, as if he'd read Adam's thoughts. "My guys brought me the rest of my gear. If you do anything stupid, I'll taze your ass."

Mason sighed. "I can't shoot him?"

"Enough of this bullshit." Adam tried to push past Jeep, but his brother had him collared before he'd taken three steps.

"I'm not going to do anything stupid," he told Jeep, toe to toe. "I just want to find Callie, damn it!"

Jeep jabbed a finger at his chest. "We don't go anywhere with our asses hanging out. Is that clear?"

Adam recognized a command when he heard one. Jeep was right. "Okay. We'll do this your way."

Nodding, Jeep took the lead down the main path, toward the entrance to the woods. "We'll switch to single file once we reach the trees."

Adam pointed his flashlight about twenty feet ahead, where twin oaks marked the easiest entrance to the woods.

Jeep tapped on his watch. "The cellar should be due north."

By unspoken agreement, they lapsed into silence. Despite his jacket and gloves, the cold pressed in around Adam, and he tamped down another surge of desperation. Callie had to be okay. He couldn't bear to think otherwise. All his energy was focused on finding her unharmed. He'd been a first-rate jerk, but she was a forgiving soul. What had happened in the past could be worked out. He'd hate himself forever if his temper tantrum had ruined their chance at happiness.

He checked his watch. They'd been walking for about five minutes. Even though every step through the dense underbrush seemed to be happening in slow mo, they were getting closer. Adam was about to say as much when Jeep stopped.

Adam stamped his feet as his older brother ran his flashlight around the underbrush, more from impatience than cold. By his count, he could keep silent for five more minutes max, then he was going to start screaming Callie's name like a wild man, danger, or no.

Jeep came full circle and met his eyes, and Adam realized he wasn't fooling anyone. Both his brothers could guess how close to the edge he was. An owl hooted above them, slicing through the eerie silence and nearly sending him into cardiac arrest.

"We should be about one click away," Jeep whispered.

"In English, please," Mason said.

"A bit more than half a mile. I'll slow down when we get close." He pointed his flashlight along the ground again. "Someone's been on this trail recently."

Adam flashed his own light around while his thoughts did a one-eighty. Thank God Jeep was in the lead. Trail? What trail? It all looked the same to Adam, towering, sharp-needled evergreens and squat, naked shrubs that speared him through his clothing.

They marched on. After a few minutes, Jeep slowed and began running his light along the ground in a zigzag pattern, left to right and back again. Adam and Mason followed suit. The flashlights illuminated the fallen leaves and pine straw, but even that wasn't enough.

A low branch sprung out of nowhere and clobbered Adam, sending him two steps backward while his flashlight rolled into the brush. "Son of a—"

"Shhh!" Jeep pointed at the beam of Adam's fallen flashlight. It highlighted a squat bush about ten feet away. "See that?"

Adam squinted, and then he saw it. A little piece of orange attached to a branch. "What is it?"

Putting his finger to his lips, Jeep crossed to the bush, moving as if he weighed nothing instead of a muscle-bound two hundred pounds, and removed the item. He returned just as noiselessly, holding out a bit of fluff.

Adam took it, crushing it in his fist as recognition dawned and adrenaline soared. "It's yarn. Callie's knitting a blanket in exactly this color." He kicked at the underbrush. "She's here. Find the doors." He fell to the ground and began scrabbling around in the leaves like a man possessed.

"Found it." Six feet away, Jeep's voice was low and in control, his light trained on a spot on the forest floor.

In seconds, he and Mason had pushed aside the dead branches and leaves to reveal the cellar doors. Adam growled in frustration when he saw they were chained shut.

Jeep reached into his back pocket, retrieved a multi-tool a little bigger than a Swiss Army knife, and flipped out a pair of bad-ass bolt cutters.

"God, I love you," Adam said fervently.

"I know." In seconds, the lock was in pieces.

Shoving his brothers aside, Adam yanked open the doors and started down the stairs.

He'd descended three when everything went black.

Chapter Seventeen

"So, *you* hit your husband over the head?" The uniformed police officer raised his eyebrows.

"Yes." Callie's gaze dropped to the officer's name badge. "Deputy Hayes. By accident. I didn't know it was him. I thought it was the kidnapper coming back. That's why I need to see him—my husband, I mean."

Edgy didn't even begin to explain her mood after nearly two hours of questioning by every agency in DC's alphabet soup. Now, it was the locals' turn. If the interrogation didn't end soon, she was going to lose it.

"And your husband is…" The young deputy flipped through his notebook. "Adam Hughes."

She clenched her jaw. To be fair, there were a lot of Hughes men running around, and the deputy was just doing his job. "That's right. Where is he? Is he okay?" She'd waited long enough.

"He's fine."

Her eyes closed, and her shoulders sagged at the sound of Adam's voice. Turning, she faced him.

The left side of his head sported a large gauze bandage, and a purple bruise discolored his temple, but aside from that, everything appeared to be in working order. For a moment, she stood there while little knives of uncertainty stabbed at her flesh. Then he threw his arms wide.

She didn't need a second invitation. Laughing, crying, and talking all at once, she dove into his embrace.

He was safe. She was safe.

She'd get a chance to make things right between them. Somehow, she'd make him understand. "I'm sorry. I'm so, so sorry. For everything."

"Shhh." His lips grazed the top of her head, her cheek, her mouth. "It's my fault."

"No, it was all me. I should have told you." His beautiful face blurred as her eyes filled with tears.

He straightened. "Officer, can you get whatever else you need from the others? This has been a harrowing ordeal for all of us, and I'd like to take my wife home now."

Home. What a wonderful word.

Unless he was talking about her apartment. The thought sent her back to shifting ground. Everything, even his kisses, could all be explained by the evening's events.

Yet he kept her tucked up against him. That had to count for something.

"Yes, sir. I think I have everything I need for now." The deputy pocketed his notebook and touched a hand to his wide hat brim in polite dismissal. "We'll be in touch."

Adam's hand slipped from her back to her waist as he led her through the crowded living room toward the front door.

"Wait. We're leaving? I haven't said goodbye to your parents."

Was it a trick of the light, or did his smile widen? He gave her a small squeeze, then released her waist to grab her hand instead. "Later. Right now, we need to talk."

Much to her surprise, he led her away from the car and down toward the river.

"Are you cold?" he asked.

"Uh, no." She was, but she was more confused and curious. Where were they going?

Then she knew. "This leads to the boathouse."

He clicked his phone flashlight on as they left the lit perimeter of the house. "That's right."

"I thought you were taking me home."

"I'm too impatient. The boathouse will do."

Impatient. She peered at him through the dark. His chin had that aggressive edge to it, and he walked purposefully, a man on a mission.

But was it one of good will?

She stumbled and he threaded his fingers more firmly through hers but kept up his pace. In another minute, they had reached the boathouse. Adam found the key, unlocked the door, then ushered her inside.

"Okay. We're here. Why are you so impa—"

Her words were swallowed by his mouth, hard and hungry against hers. Hands groping, lips seeking, she poured every pent-up emotion she'd experienced over the past several hours into her response. Finally, by unspoken agreement, they separated, but only by scant inches, both disheveled and breathing hard.

"My hero." Callie touched the bruise on Adam's forehead with shaky fingers and managed a small laugh. "This will teach you not to go charging in like a madman to save the day."

He led her over to the stairs. "I agree. I should have known better than to think you needed saving." He waved her up the winding staircase. "Lucky for me the log you clobbered me with was mostly rotten, Wonder Woman," he said, following her up.

At the top of the stairs, he swung her around for

another kiss. This one was softer, forgiving, healing.

"I'm sorry I hit you. I was so sure it was the guy coming back." Her voice faltered. "I was so scared."

He cupped her cheeks, his eyes taking on an intense look. "I love you, Cal. It's cliché as hell, but you're my everything. When I thought I'd lost you…"

Her heart swelled to the point of bursting, and she took a shaky breath, bringing her body in contact with his. "I'm stubborn and proud and too independent for my own good, but I love you, too. More than I ever dreamed I could love anyone. And I knew, no matter how upset you were, you'd come looking for me, wouldn't stop until you'd found me." She met his gaze, her own eyesight blurry with unshed tears. "It was wonderful to know I had someone in my corner. I've never felt like that before."

He rubbed his thumb along her bottom lip before leaning down for another kiss. "I know what it took for you to say that, and I thank you for the gift. For all the gifts you've given me through the years. We've both lost a hell of a lot, and I want to know all about what happened, what you went through. But I want you to know, despite all the loss, what we've gained is immeasurable. I promise, I'll never turn my back on it again."

Grabbing her hands, he guided her over to an old but sturdy-looking armchair. With frantic movements, they removed a pile of junk from its seat.

"Careful. I might want to sort through some of that later." She smiled up into his eyes.

"It's yours." Adam sat first and tugged her onto his lap. "Anything you want."

"I only want you."

He kissed her again, at first tender, then with passion, as if memorizing the taste and texture of her lips, teeth, and tongue.

"Mmmm." She chuckled as the kiss ended. "I still can't believe this is happening. That it's real. I've loved you from the start. Long before I admitted it to myself. Maybe that's why I couldn't tell you the truth about the accident."

Adam shook his head. "I was being selfish, only looking at things from my perspective. I understand now what a difficult time it must have been for you. How hard it was for you to face me, let alone come and work beside me every day." He followed the curve of her bad hip with a hand. "You're a strong woman, Callie. A survivor in so many ways, it humbles me."

She blushed. Accepting compliments was still difficult for her, but life with Adam Hughes might change that. "I just did what I had to do, whatever seemed right at the time. I've made a lot of mistakes."

He placed a finger over her mouth, shushing her. "Very few, as far as I can see. It took real courage to approach Mallory's parents after the accident. If you still want to speak with them, I'd be happy to facilitate a meeting. I think they're ready for that now. We're *all* ready for that now."

The offer touched Callie, and she dotted his face with a few kisses. "Thank you. I might take you up on that. Right now, I think we should concentrate on us. We have plenty to talk about."

He gave her a wide smile, and her heart flipped. "Agreed. We haven't had a honeymoon yet. Name the place and we'll go."

She leaned back in his arms, a mock frown on her

face. "You aren't going to start spoiling me, are you? I mean, I might grow all whiny and demanding, and then where will you be?"

His smile grew into one of his wonderful, heartfelt laughs, and he gave her another squeeze. "I like my chances. There's not a single whiny bone in this luscious body." He waggled his eyebrows. "I oughta know."

"Oh!" Her breath caught as Adam's hand found one of her more erogenous spots.

"I love you, Mrs. Hughes." His breath was hot in her ear, his voice already strained.

"I love you, too." She gasped again, as he stroked, cupped, and stroked again. *Sweet heaven.* "Are you thinking what I'm thinking?"

His mouth curved against her throat. "There's probably a bed up here somewhere."

She giggled. "I don't know that we need one. This chair's pretty big."

His hands tunneled under her sweater. "I'm up for it," he growled.

"Oh, yeah?" She dug her fingers into his back. "Prove it."

He did.

****

"Let me see if I've got this straight. First, you managed to pull the loop from the ceiling. Then, when you couldn't open the doors, you were prepared to conk the damn son of a bitch over the head?" Adam's father shook his head, admiration shining in his eyes as he looked at Adam. "I think she's a keeper, son."

Adam gave Callie's shoulders a squeeze and met her gaze with what he suspected was a silly, lovesick look on his face. He didn't care. "I know she is, Dad, even if

I'm the damn son of a bitch she nailed."

They were cuddled together on a loveseat in his parents' warm, inviting family room, where he and Callie had spent the last twenty minutes fielding the countless questions his family and Gretchen had stored up for them overnight.

His mother entered from the kitchen, carrying a tray of cinnamon-smelling coffee cake and a large pot of tea. Gretchen followed in her wake with a stack of small plates and forks. True to form, Minna shot her first born a meaningful glance and Jeep, after exchanging an amused look with the room's other occupants, responded by hopping up and relieving his mother of the tray.

"Thank you, dear." His mum sank onto the overstuffed couch with her usual distracted air. "I still can't believe this whole nightmare started because of a magazine article about a family legend. Oh, bother. I've forgotten the sugar. Gretchen, be a darling and go grab the sugar bowl, please."

Gretchen, with obvious pride, ran back into the kitchen to do Adam's mother's bidding.

"I guess someone thinks even the chance of finding a Gutenberg Bible is worth it." Priss, sitting with Mason at the other end of the large couch, gave Callie a shaky smile. "I'm so glad you're okay."

"Well, whoever that someone is, it's not the same guy who kidnapped Callie last night," Jeep said, looking at his phone.

"What do you mean?" Mason and Adam asked together.

"Sheriff Jones just emailed me. The guy we nabbed last night? There's no doubt he was the guy behind the break-ins and assaults, as well as the kidnapping. Fits the physical description to a T. His name's Anderson, Justin Anderson, and he's wanted in connection with a few jewelry store robberies. He was scared shitless and refused to talk, not that it did him much good. They found him stabbed to death in his cell half an hour ago."

Adam hugged Callie closer. "Could it be self-inflicted?" he asked.

"No chance," Jeep said.

Patrick paused in the act of resurrecting his discarded newspaper from the arm of his reading chair. "This is insane. I'll speak to the sheriff about hiring some extra protection around here." He raised a hand. "I'm serious, Min. As of right now, you don't go anywhere by yourself," he added, as his wife scowled.

"Oh, very well. I suppose you're right," Adam's mother agreed with a flick of her hand. It was clear she wasn't happy about having her wings clipped, but she'd make the best of it. "That applies to all of us." She looked around the room. "I do hope last night is the end to anymore heroics. That goes double for you, John."

"What?" Jeep sat straighter in his chair, an innocent look on his face. "I'm a lawyer. Yesterday was a one-and-done kind of thing. Always happy to help, but that's the end of it."

"Does that mean you're giving up your duffel bag?" Mason asked.

Jeep scoffed. "Let's keep my duffel out of it."

"What's in the duffel bag?" Callie wanted to know.

Leaning down, Adam kissed the spot on her temple where wisps of her beautiful, unruly hair always escaped. "I'll explain later." He cleared his throat. "For the record, I agree with Dad and Mum. This whole thing is a shi—"

"Shivering shoe," Mason interrupted, as Gretchen

re-entered the room, carrying the sugar bowl with a surfeit of concentration.

Adam acknowledged the assist with a grin before growing serious again. "I don't think any of us can be too careful until this whole thing is cleared up."

Beside him, Callie nodded. "Anderson was terrified of whoever is calling the shots. The reason he resorted to kidnapping was because he was in way over his head."

"In the meantime, what if I hire a professional to come in and look for the Bible? Don't get me wrong, I'm still nowhere near convinced it's a Gutenberg," Patrick said, around a droopy corner of his paper. "But having a professional perform an exhaustive search should put an end to the whole thing. You know more than a few commando types, Jeep. Are you in touch with any treasure hunters, too?"

Jeep grimaced. "You guys insist on painting me as some kind of Rambo, don't you?"

Mason shrugged. "If the biceps match…"

"As it happens," Jeep said, speaking over Mason, "I do know a woman who does that sort of thing."

"Ooh, a Rambette."

"Don't be sexist, dear," Minna told Mason.

"Sorry, Mum," Mason said.

"Is a Rambette like a unicorn?" Gretchen asked, raising another wave of laughter.

Callie touched her forehead to Adam's. "Thank you," she whispered.

"For what?" he whispered back.

She tilted her head toward the rest of the room. "For this."

A lump formed in Adam's throat as he soaked up the good-natured bickering going on around them. "They each have their own kind of crazy, but I'm happy to share them with you."

"Promise?"

He smiled. "I promise," he whispered against her lips.

And he sealed that promise with a kiss.

Epilogue

"Oooh! What about this old artist's colony in Washington State? These cabins look awesome, plus there's a pottery studio! When I'm not researching, I can get in a little time at the wheel." Callie handed Adam the tablet, waiting while he browsed the website.

They snuggled on the couch in the study, by a blazing fire and a twinkling tree, full of Minna's amazing Christmas morning brunch, as the season's first true snowstorm blew outside.

"The four-bedroom looks like it would have plenty of room for all of us," he said, scrolling through the floorplan.

"You're sure you want to bring Gretchen and Eloise along?" The thought of leaving her sister behind for the entire summer was impossible to imagine, but peace and quiet had always been an essential part of Adam's annual summer retreat, and Gretchen, God love her, wasn't very good at either.

"Absolutely sure. It'll be fun. Plus, I'll need Gretchen's help with the book," he said, giving her a wink.

"Only if it's the *right* kind of book," Gretchen reminded him as she walked past the couch, her eyes glued to the steaming mug of hot chocolate and homemade marshmallows she carried.

He gave her one of his megawatt smiles. "We'll

see."

God, he was adorable. Callie leaned over and kissed him. Mindful of their audience, the smooch was quick, but hinted at things to come.

"You're spending tonight here too, aren't you?" Her mother-in-law was reading in one of the two armchairs, her feet propped close to the fire, wire-rimmed cheaters listing dangerously on the tip of her nose.

"Yes." Callie exchanged a smile with her husband. She could tell he got a kick out of how much she was enjoying her first real family holiday. "We wouldn't miss it."

"May have to get the plow out, if this keeps up." Patrick released the wooden blind and reclaimed the other armchair before disappearing behind his open newspaper.

"Don't you think you can let the security crew go home, dear? There's been no sign of trouble since the kidnapping, and it's Christmas, after all."

Patrick lowered a corner of his paper. "That's exactly why I'm *not* letting them go. I want the peace to continue. But I'll give them a generous Christmas bonus, if that'll make you feel better. And some of your Christmas pudding."

"Hey." Mason breezed into the room, Priss's mittened hand wrapped in his. "Sorry we're late. Just got off shift." He tugged off a snow-dotted woolen hat. "Damn, it's coming down out there. Is there anything left to eat? I'm starving."

"So, help me, if you eat something with Dijon mustard on it, I'll beat you," Jeep threatened, without raising his head from the jigsaw puzzle he, Gretchen, and Eloise were busy working on.

"No promises," Mason said, releasing his wife and heading for the kitchen.

Priss jumped as her phone chimed and glanced down at the screen. "Oh. Excuse me. I'll be right back," she said, as she slipped from the room.

"How much do you wanna bet Mason brings back a sandwich slathered in mustard?" Adam breathed into Callie's ear, sending sparks of desire coursing through her body. It should be illegal how sexy this man was.

She looped her arms around his neck as he leaned in for another tempting taste.

"No bet." She giggled. "You know he's coming back with mustard. Even if he has to slather it on coffee cake."

"Mmm." Adam kissed her nose. "You know our family so well."

Callie smiled and rested her head on his shoulder. "Shimmering salamanders. You say the nicest things."

A word about the author...

Eva Fox Mate has been writing ever since she could hold a pencil. An avid reader, crafter, and lover of history, when she isn't writing or volunteering at a house museum, she's wielding a crochet hook or glue gun and looking for something to DIY.

A transplanted Ohioan, she now lives in the Mile High City of Denver, Colorado, with her husband of over 30 wonderful years. Empty nesters, they enjoy golfing, traveling, and spending time with their two adult children and their two zany and much-spoiled dogs.

Visit her at:

evafoxmate.com